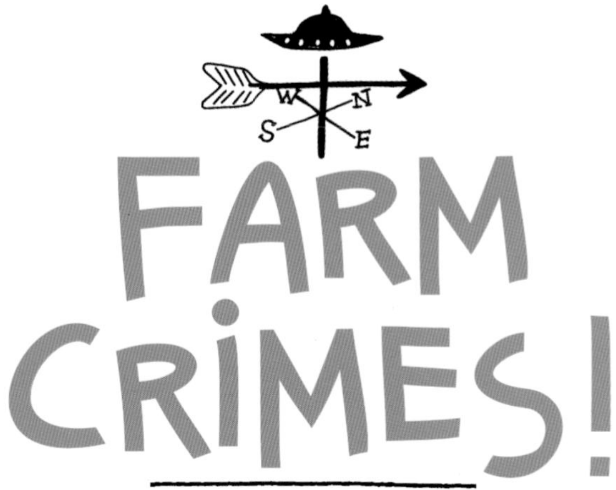
W
N
S
E

FARM CRIMES!

THE MOO-STERIOUS DISAPPEARANCE OF COW

Sandra Dumais

OWLKIDS BOOKS

It was a beautiful afternoon on the farm. Fall was in the air.

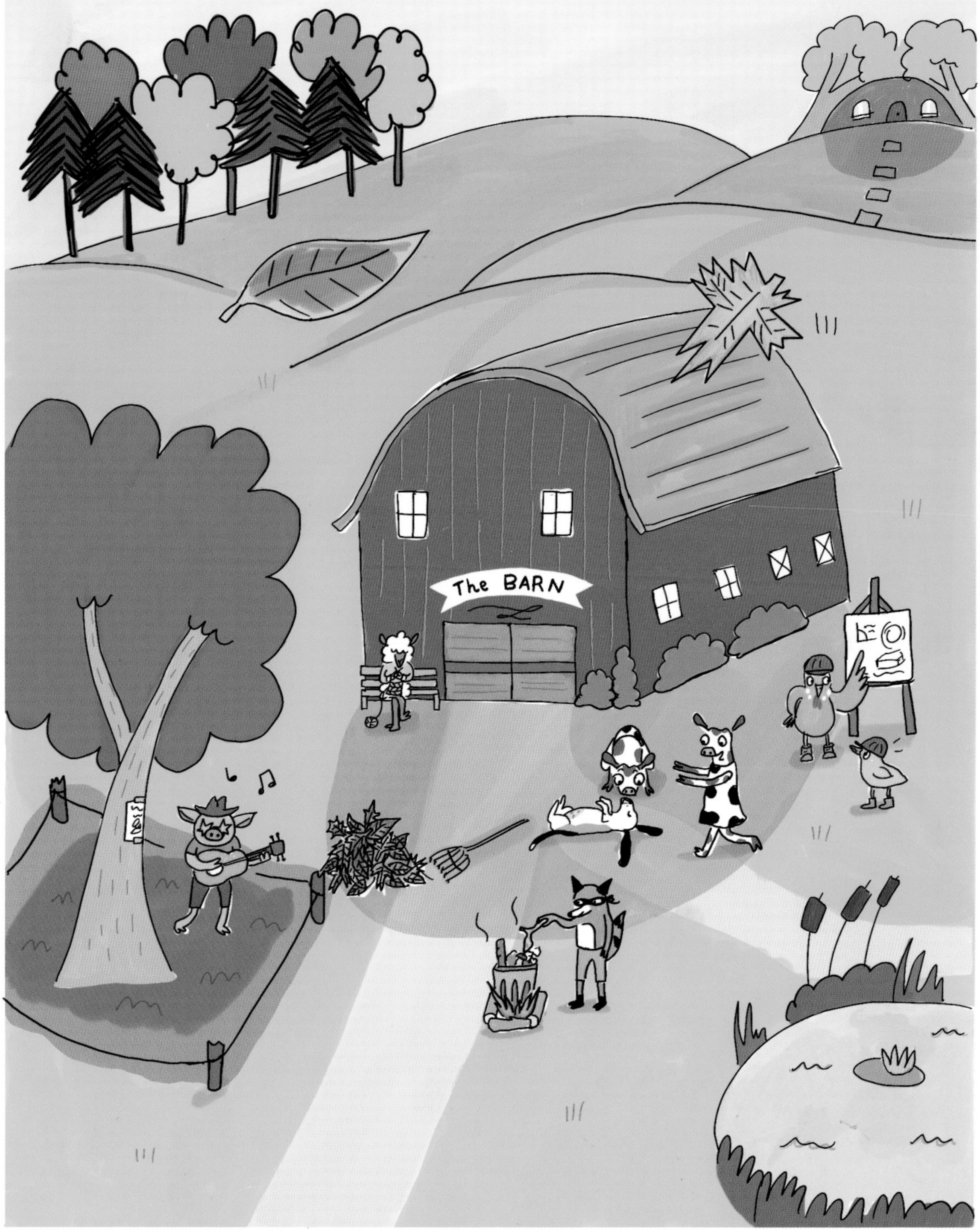
The BARN

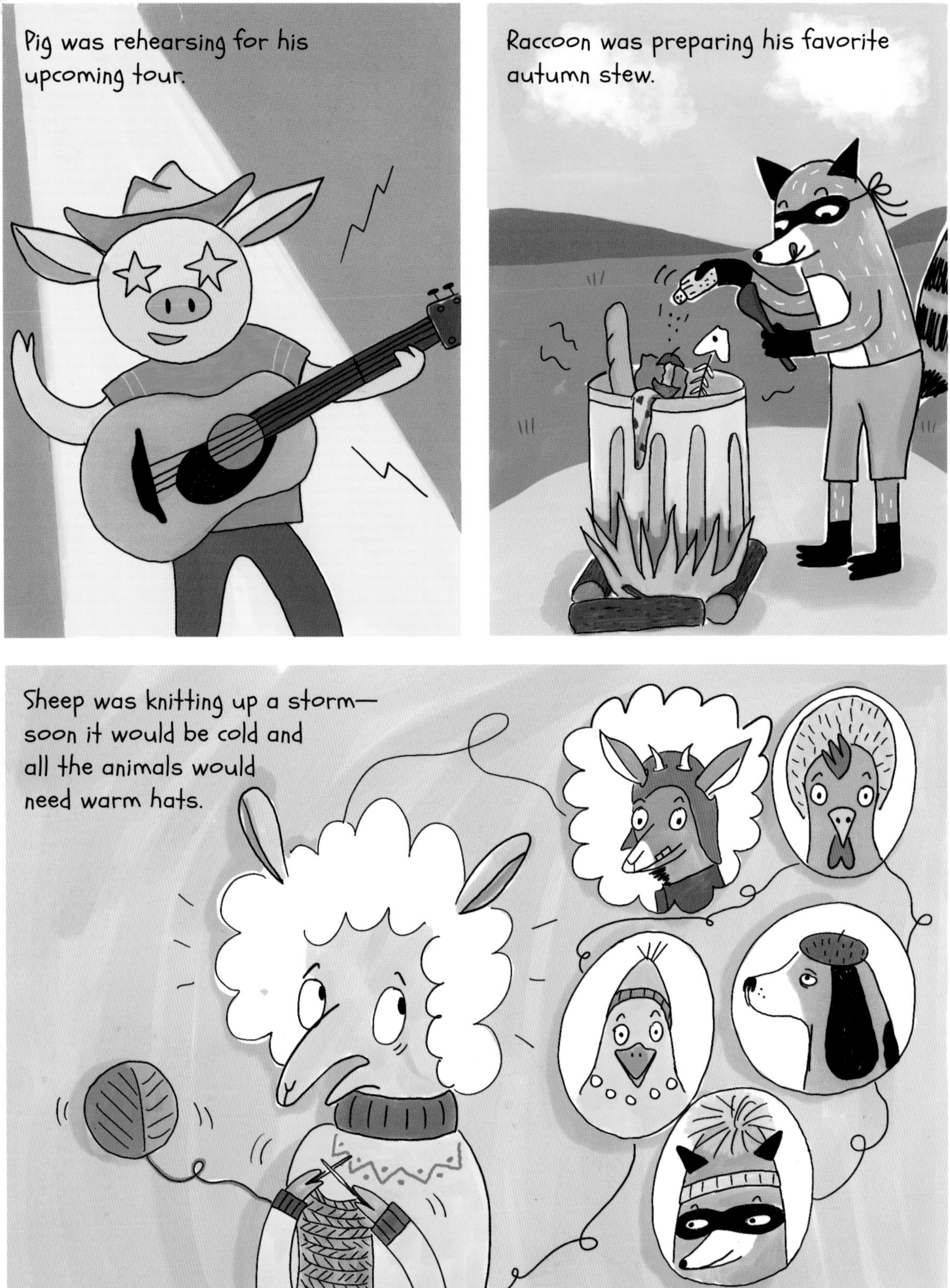
Pig was rehearsing for his upcoming tour.
Raccoon was preparing his favorite autumn stew.
Sheep was knitting up a storm— soon it would be cold and all the animals would need warm hats.

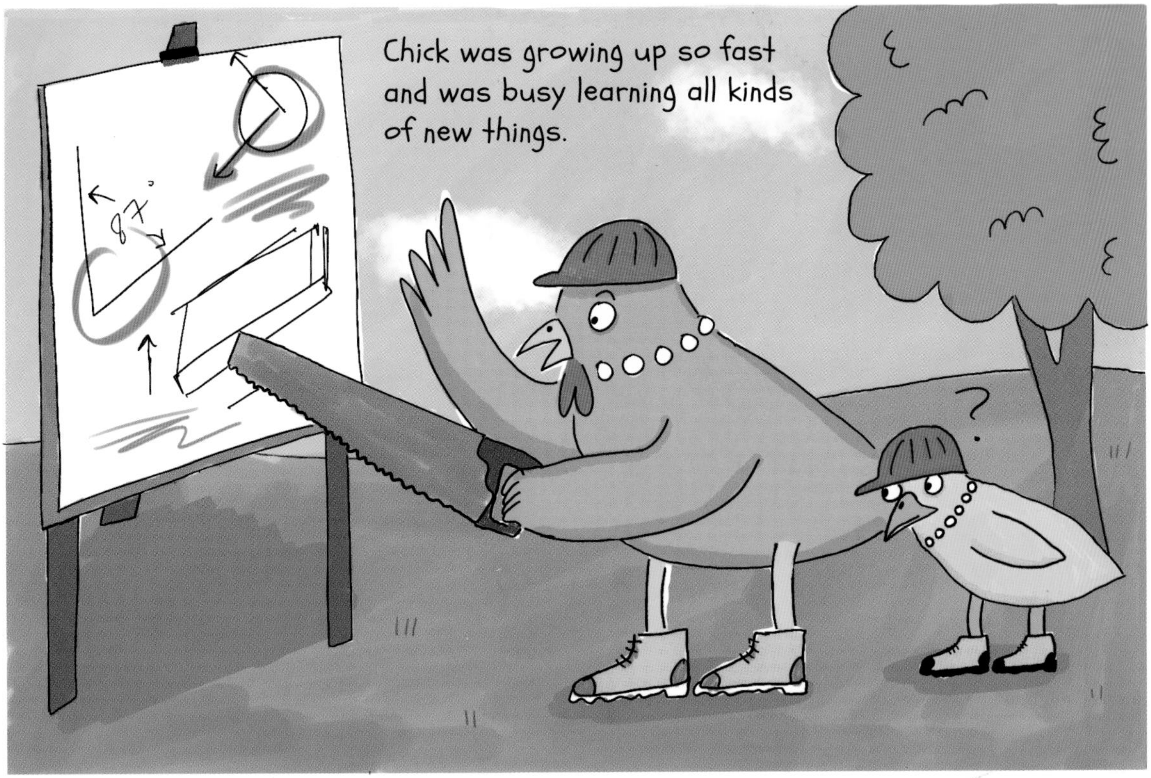
Chick was growing up so fast and was busy learning all kinds of new things.
87°
?

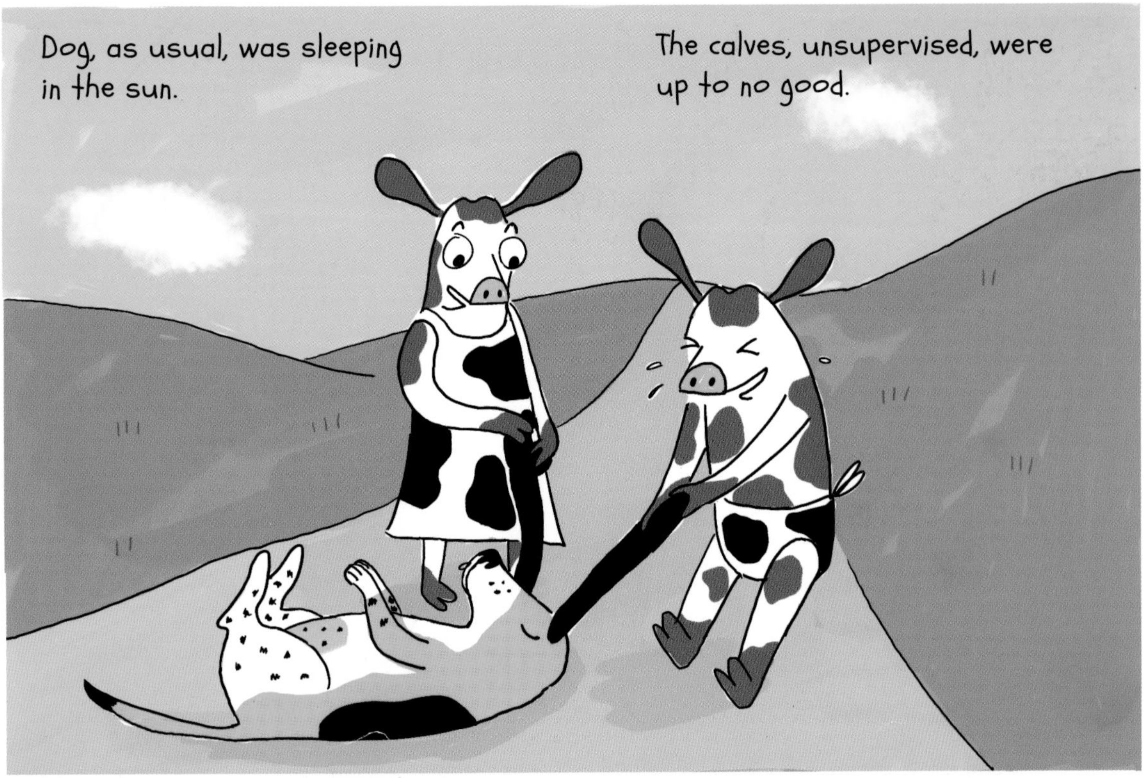
Dog, as usual, was sleeping in the sun.
The calves, unsupervised, were up to no good.

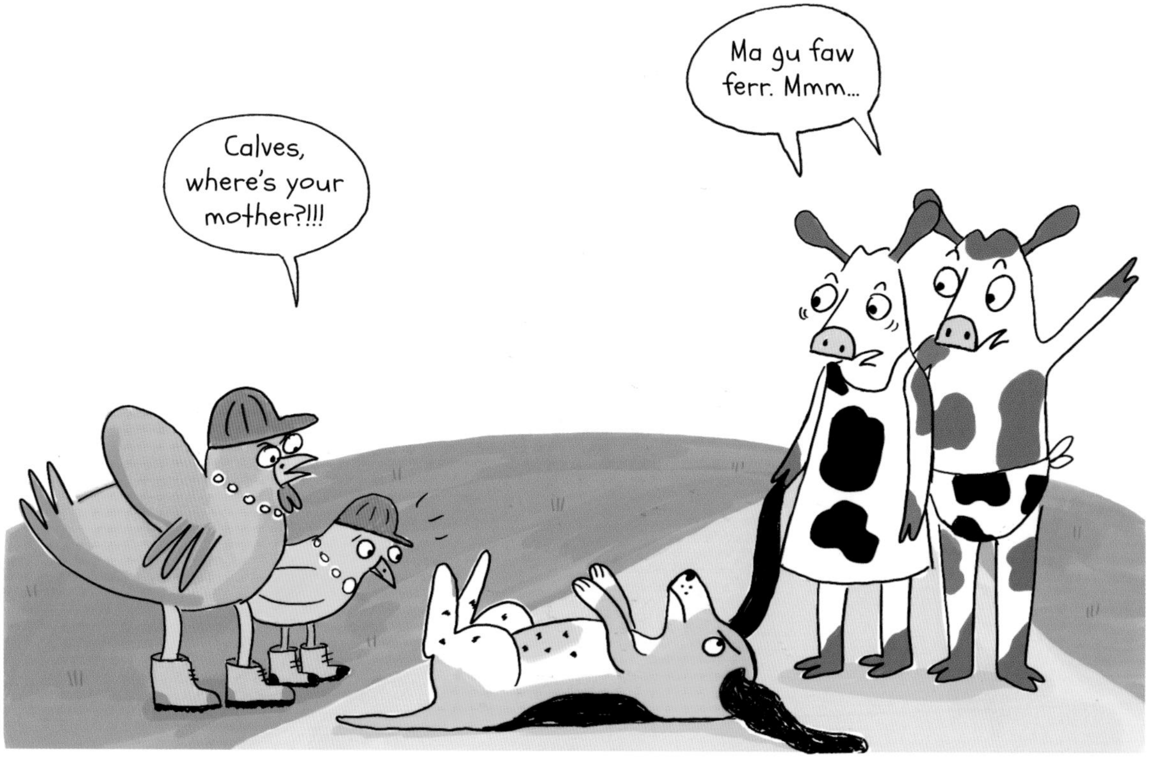
Calves, where's your mother?!!!
Ma gu faw ferr. Mmm...

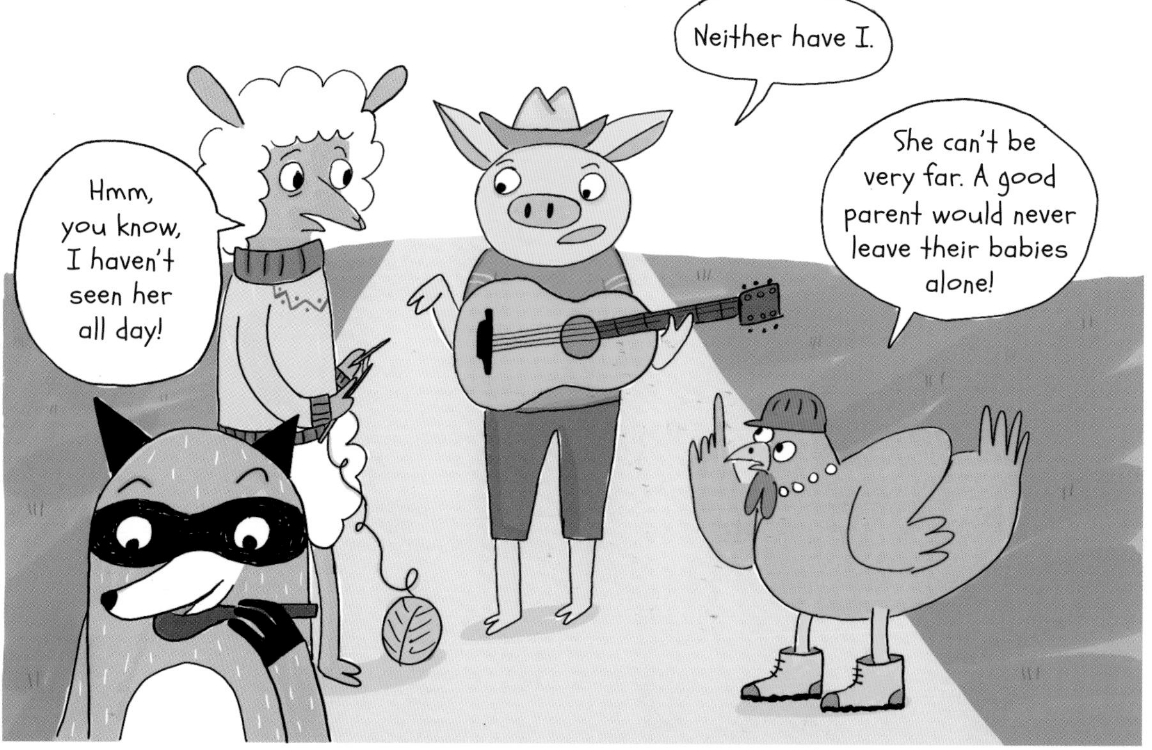
Hmm, you know, I haven't seen her all day!
Neither have I.
She can't be very far. A good parent would never leave their babies alone!

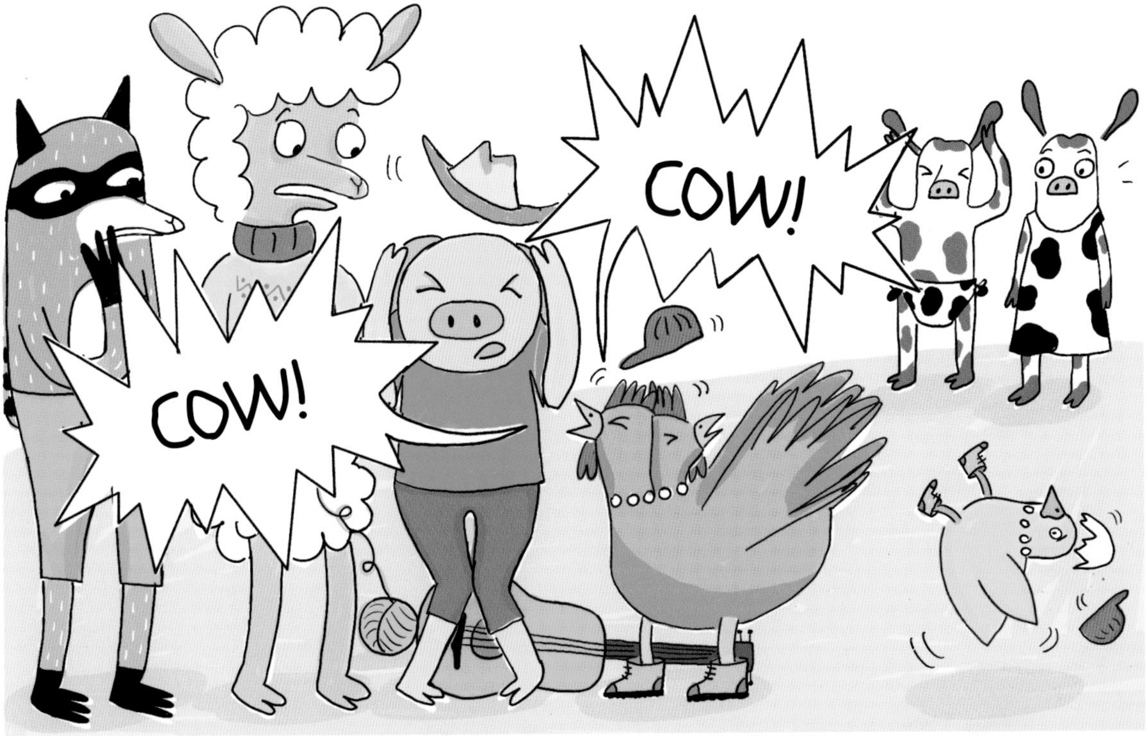
COW!
COW!

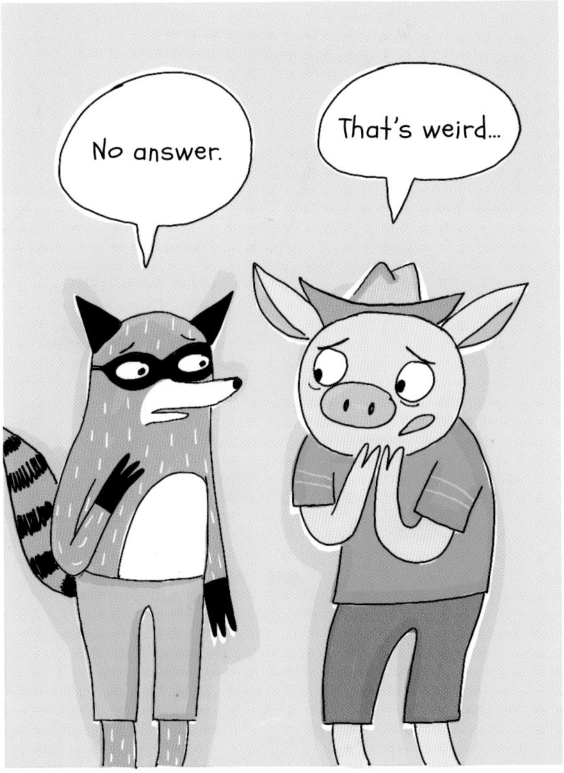
No answer.
That's weird...

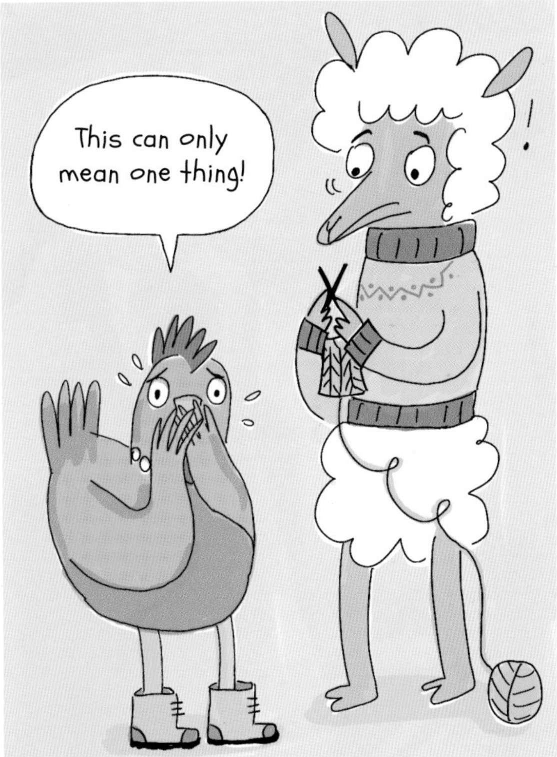
This can only mean one thing!

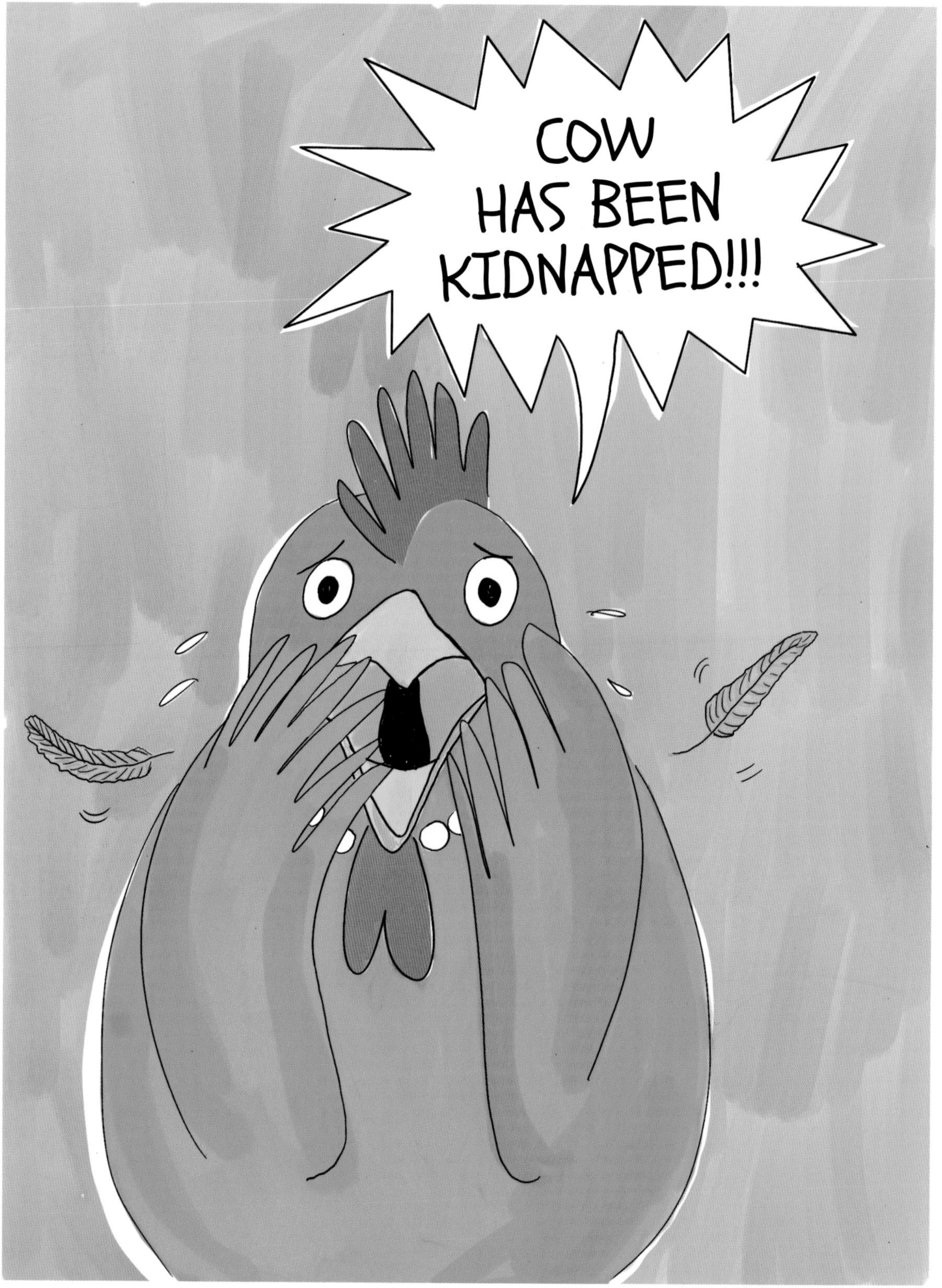
COW
HAS BEEN
KIDNAPPED!!!

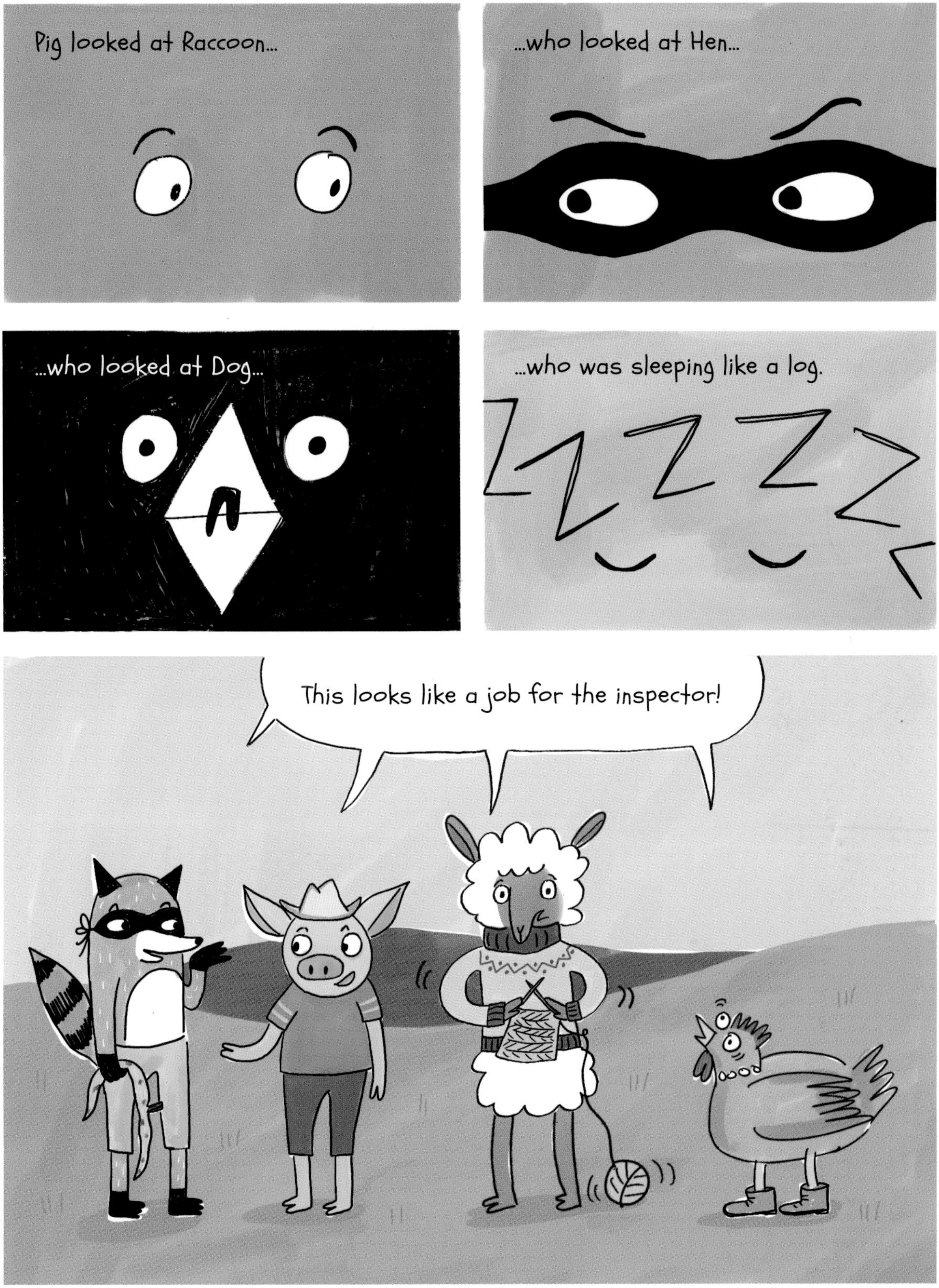
Pig looked at Raccoon...
...who looked at Hen...
...who looked at Dog...
...who was sleeping like a log.
This looks like a job for the inspector!

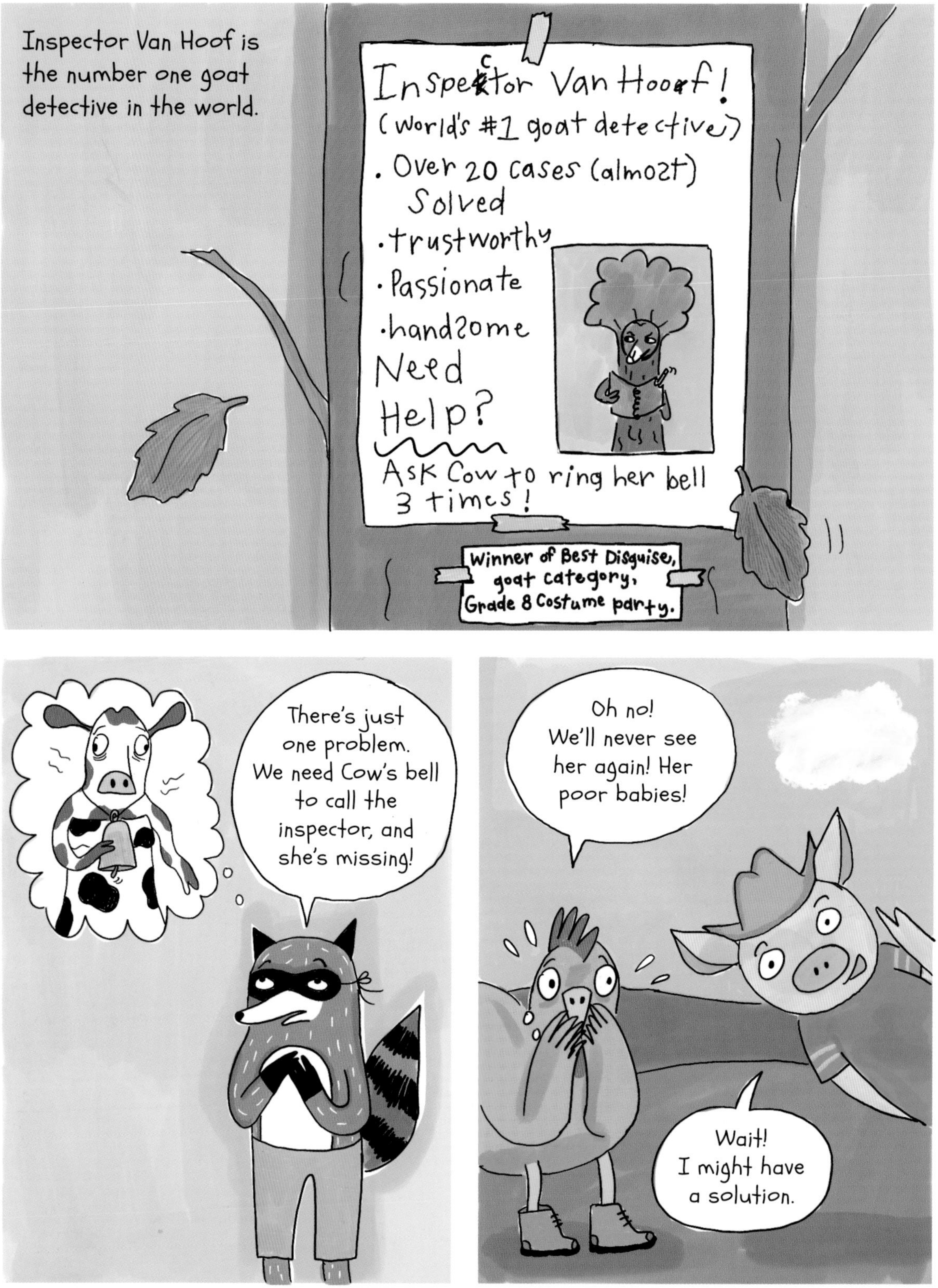
Inspector Van Hoof is the number one goat detective in the world.
Inspector Van Hoof!
(World's #1 goat detective)
. Over 20 cases (almozt) Solved
. trustworthy
. Passionate
. handzome
Need Help?
Ask Cow to ring her bell 3 times!
Winner of Best Disguise, goat category, Grade 8 Costume party.
There's just one problem. We need Cow's bell to call the inspector, and she's missing!
Oh no! We'll never see her again! Her poor babies!
Wait! I might have a solution.

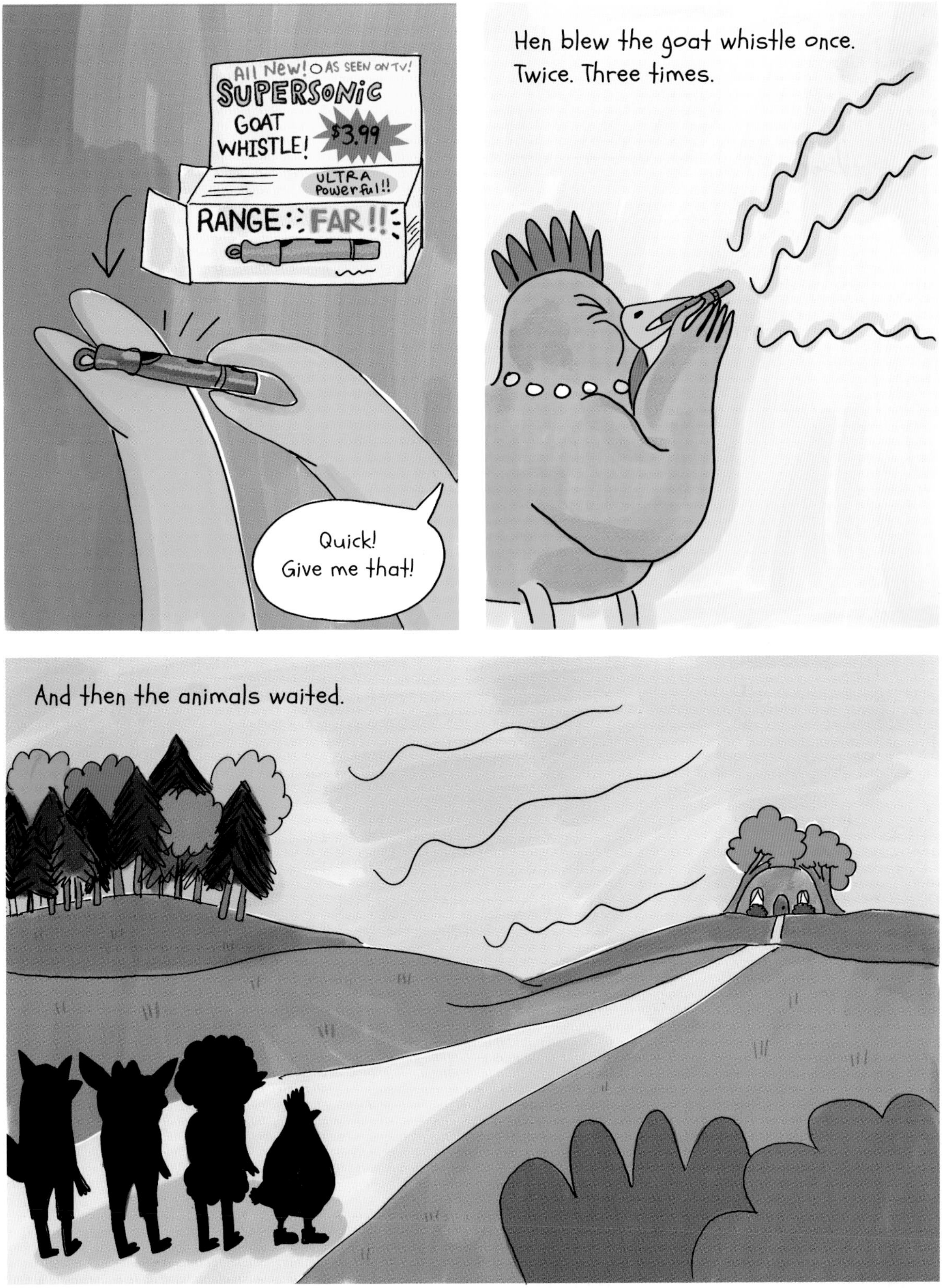

All New!
AS SEEN ON TV!
SUPERSONIC GOAT WHISTLE!
$3.99
ULTRA Powerful!!
RANGE: FAR!!
Quick! Give me that!
Hen blew the goat whistle once. Twice. Three times.
And then the animals waited.

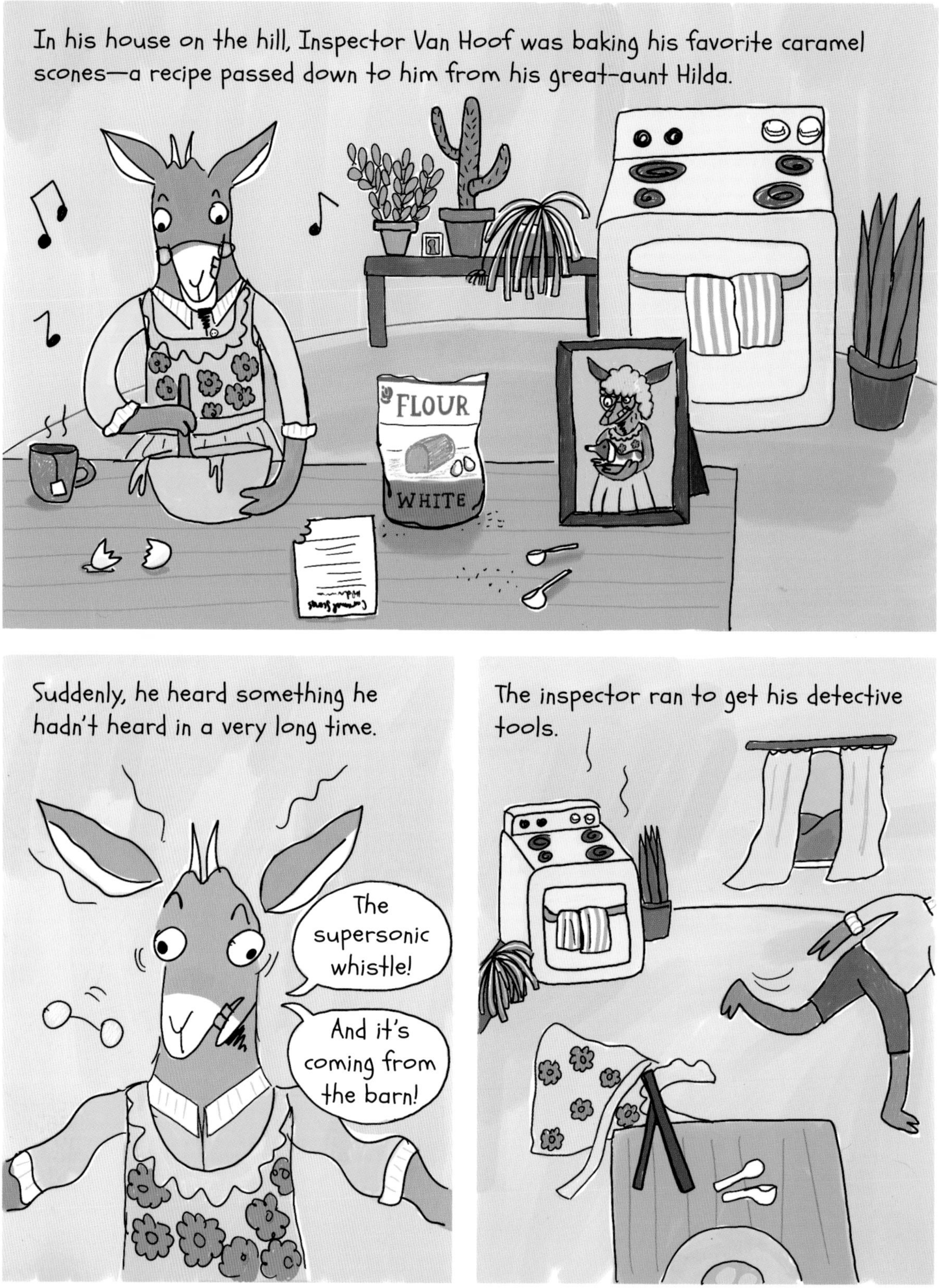
In his house on the hill, Inspector Van Hoof was baking his favorite caramel scones—a recipe passed down to him from his great-aunt Hilda.
FLOUR
WHITE
Suddenly, he heard something he hadn't heard in a very long time.
The supersonic whistle!
And it's coming from the barn!
The inspector ran to get his detective tools.

He prepared for (almost) every scenario...

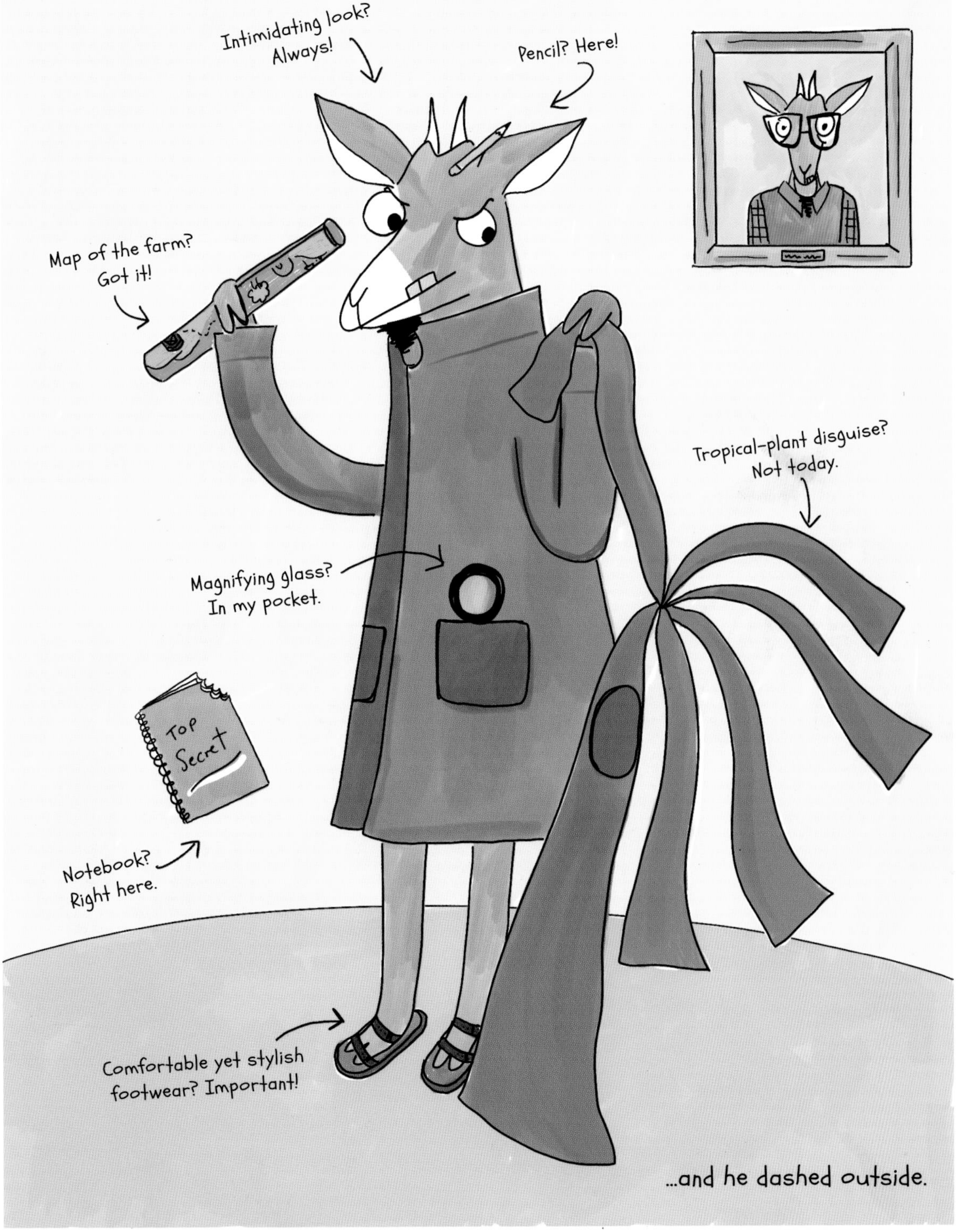

Intimidating look? Always!
Pencil? Here!
Map of the farm? Got it!
Tropical-plant disguise? Not today.
Magnifying glass? In my pocket.
Top Secret
Notebook? Right here.
Comfortable yet stylish footwear? Important!

...and he dashed outside.

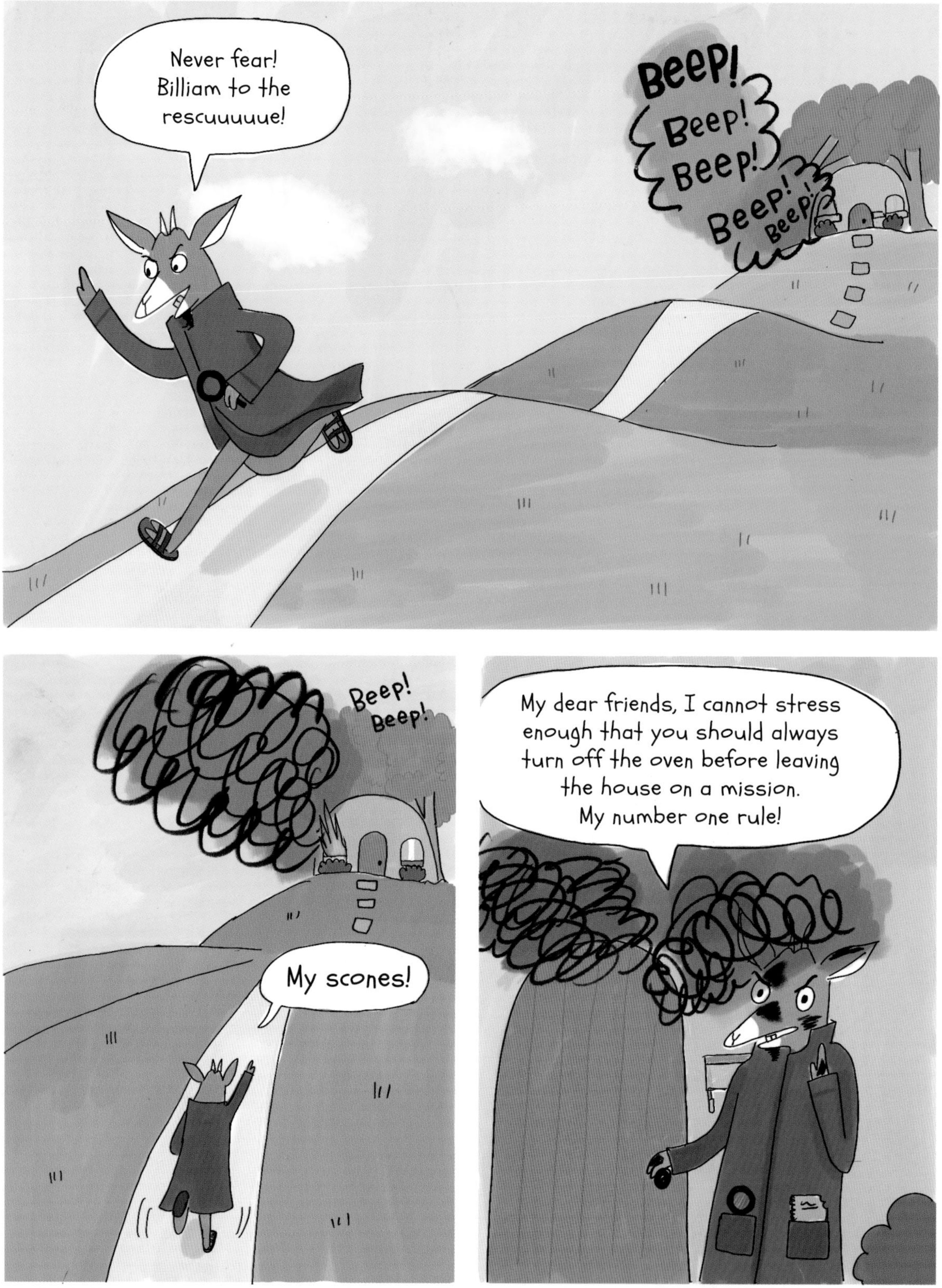
Never fear! Billiam to the rescuuuuue!
BEEP!
Beep!
Beep!
Beep!
Beep!
Beep!
Beep!
Beep!
My scones!
My dear friends, I cannot stress enough that you should always turn off the oven before leaving the house on a mission. My number one rule!

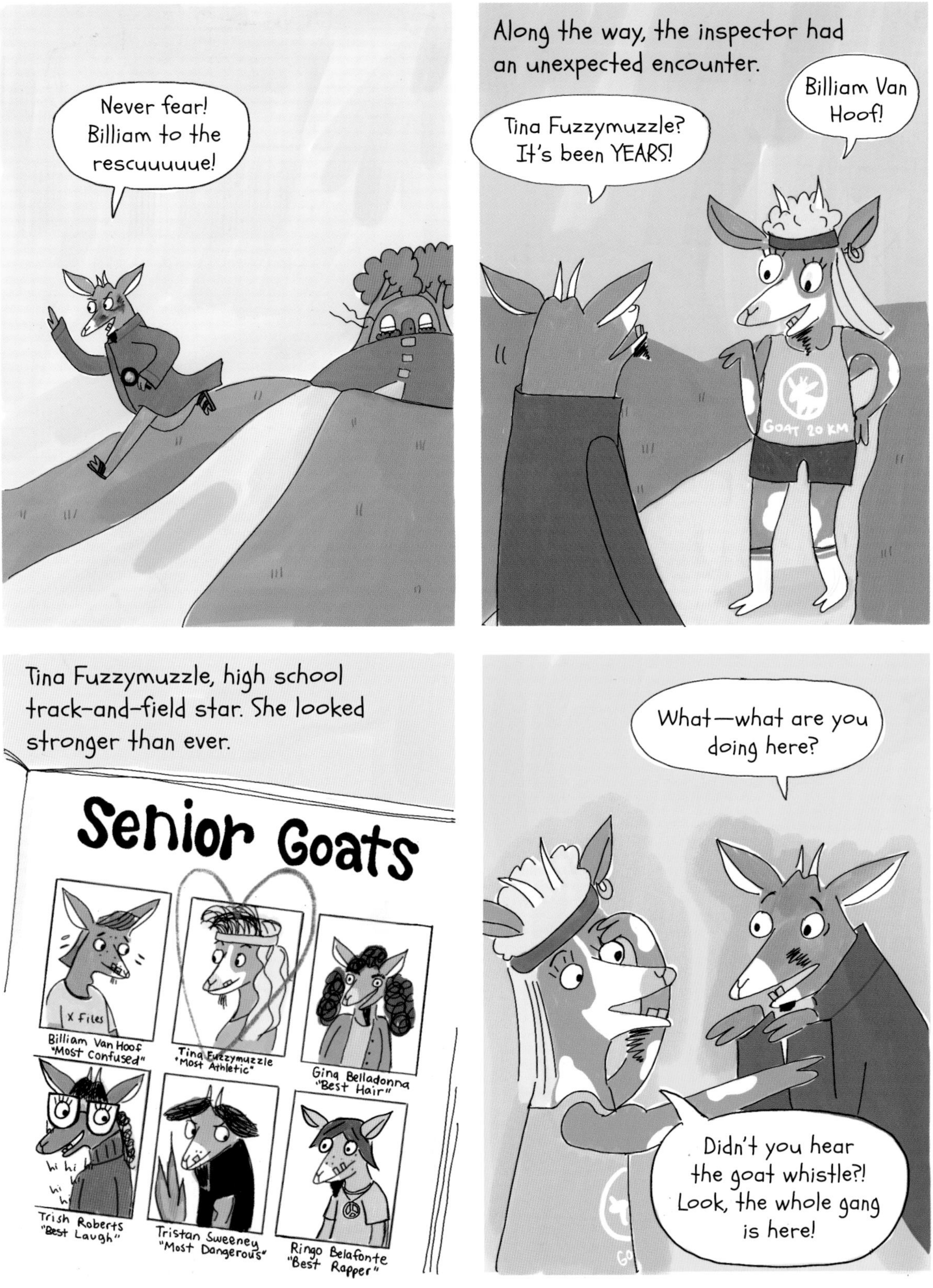
Never fear! Billiam to the rescuuuuue!
Along the way, the inspector had an unexpected encounter.
Tina Fuzzymuzzle? It's been YEARS!
Billiam Van Hoof!
GOAT 20 KM
Tina Fuzzymuzzle, high school track-and-field star. She looked stronger than ever.
Senior Goats
X Files
Billiam Van Hoof "Most Confused"
Tina Fuzzymuzzle "Most Athletic"
Gina Belladonna "Best Hair"
Trish Roberts "Best Laugh"
Tristan Sweeney "Most Dangerous"
Ringo Belafonte "Best Rapper"
What—what are you doing here?
Didn't you hear the goat whistle?! Look, the whole gang is here!

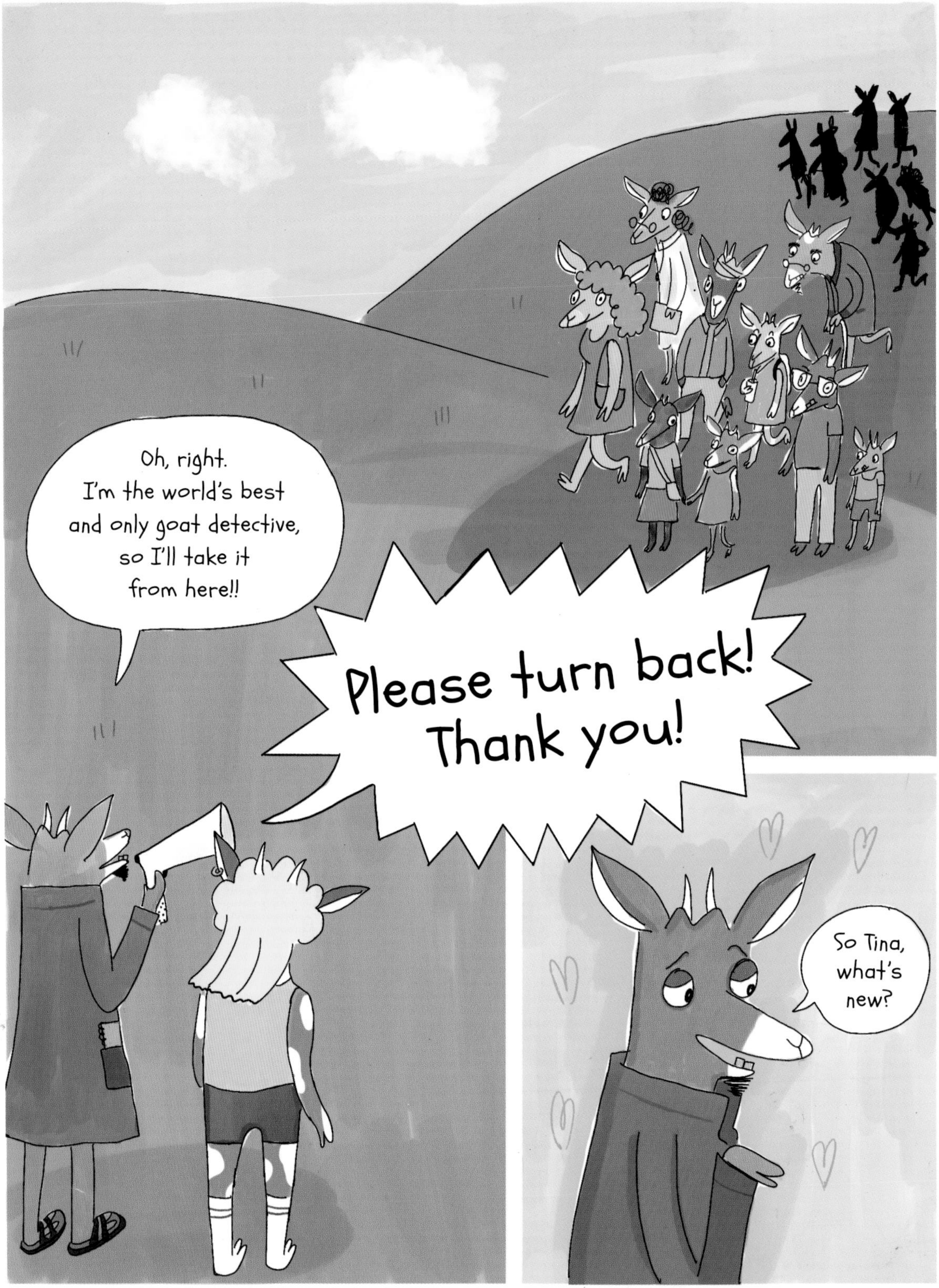
Oh, right. I'm the world's best and only goat detective, so I'll take it from here!!
Please turn back! Thank you!
So Tina, what's new?

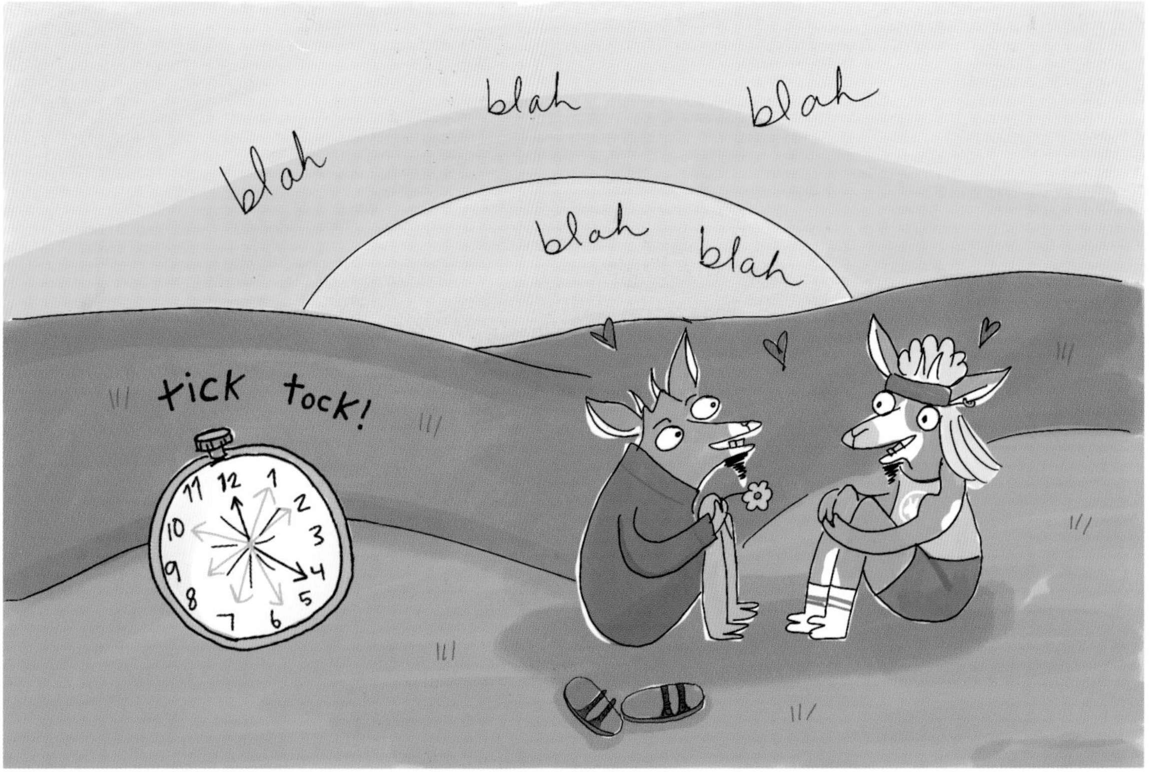
blah
blah
blah
blah
blah
tick tock!

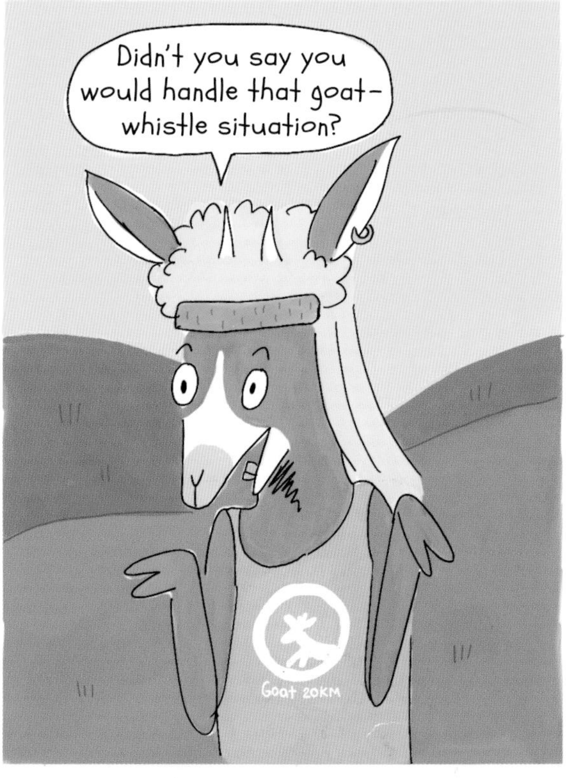
Didn't you say you would handle that goat-whistle situation?
Goat 20KM

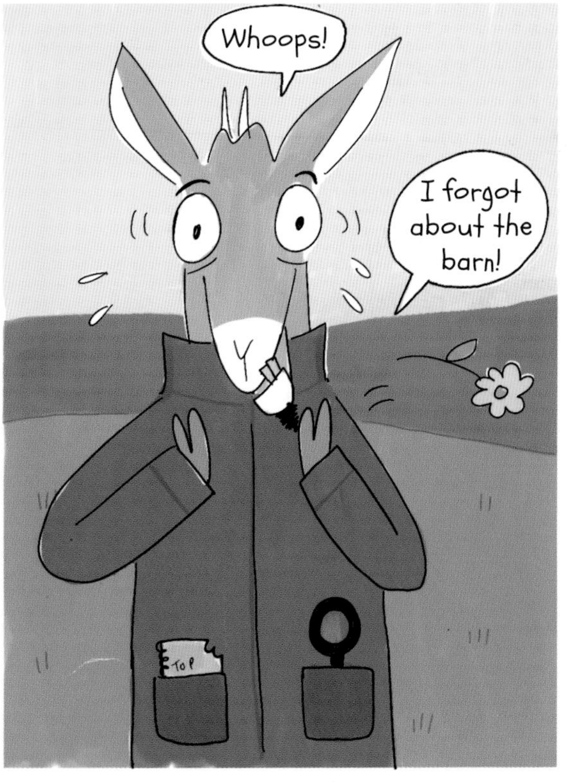
Whoops!
I forgot about the barn!
TOP

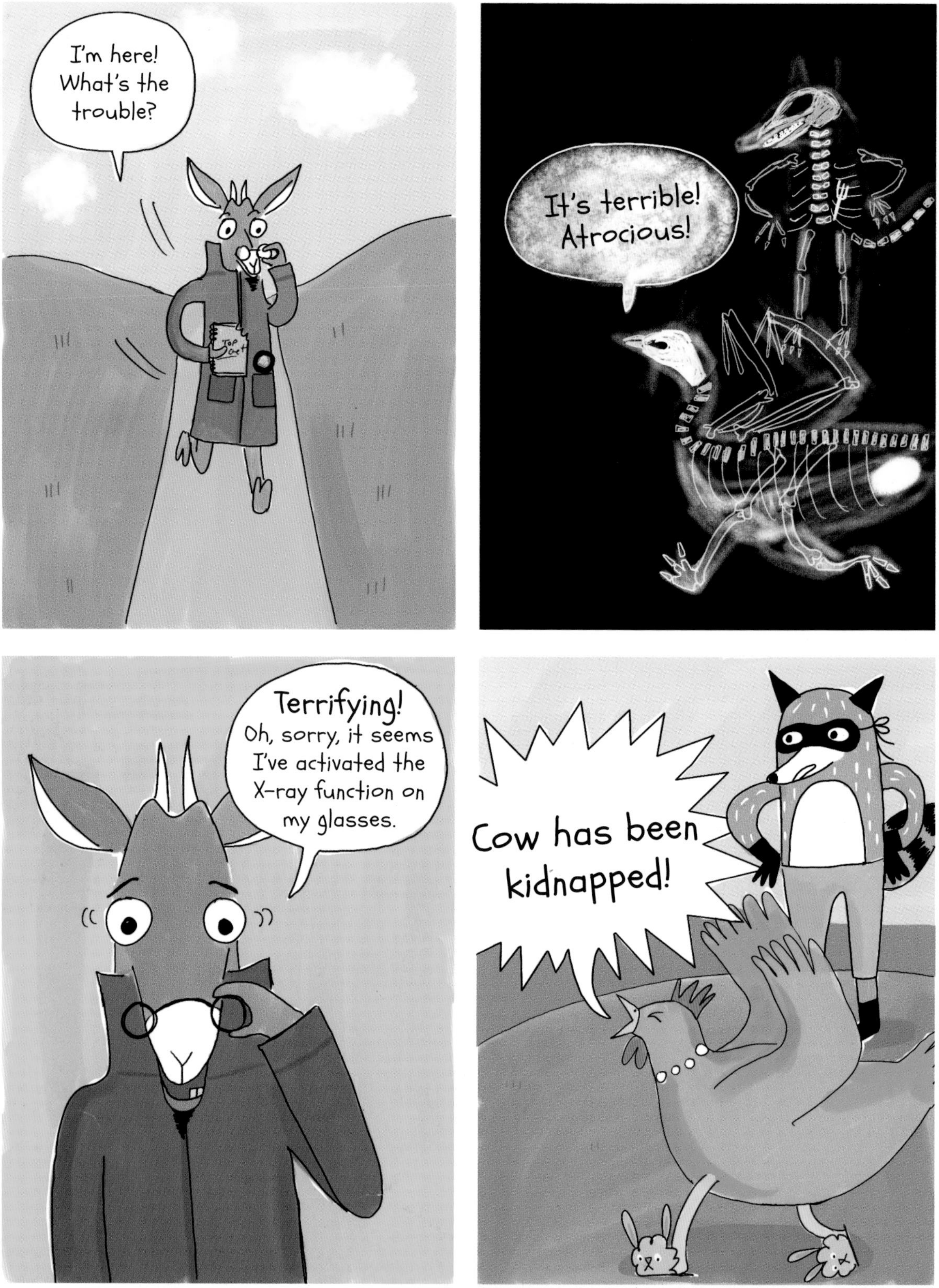
I'm here! What's the trouble?
Top Secret
It's terrible! Atrocious!
Terrifying! Oh, sorry, it seems I've activated the X-ray function on my glasses.
Cow has been kidnapped!

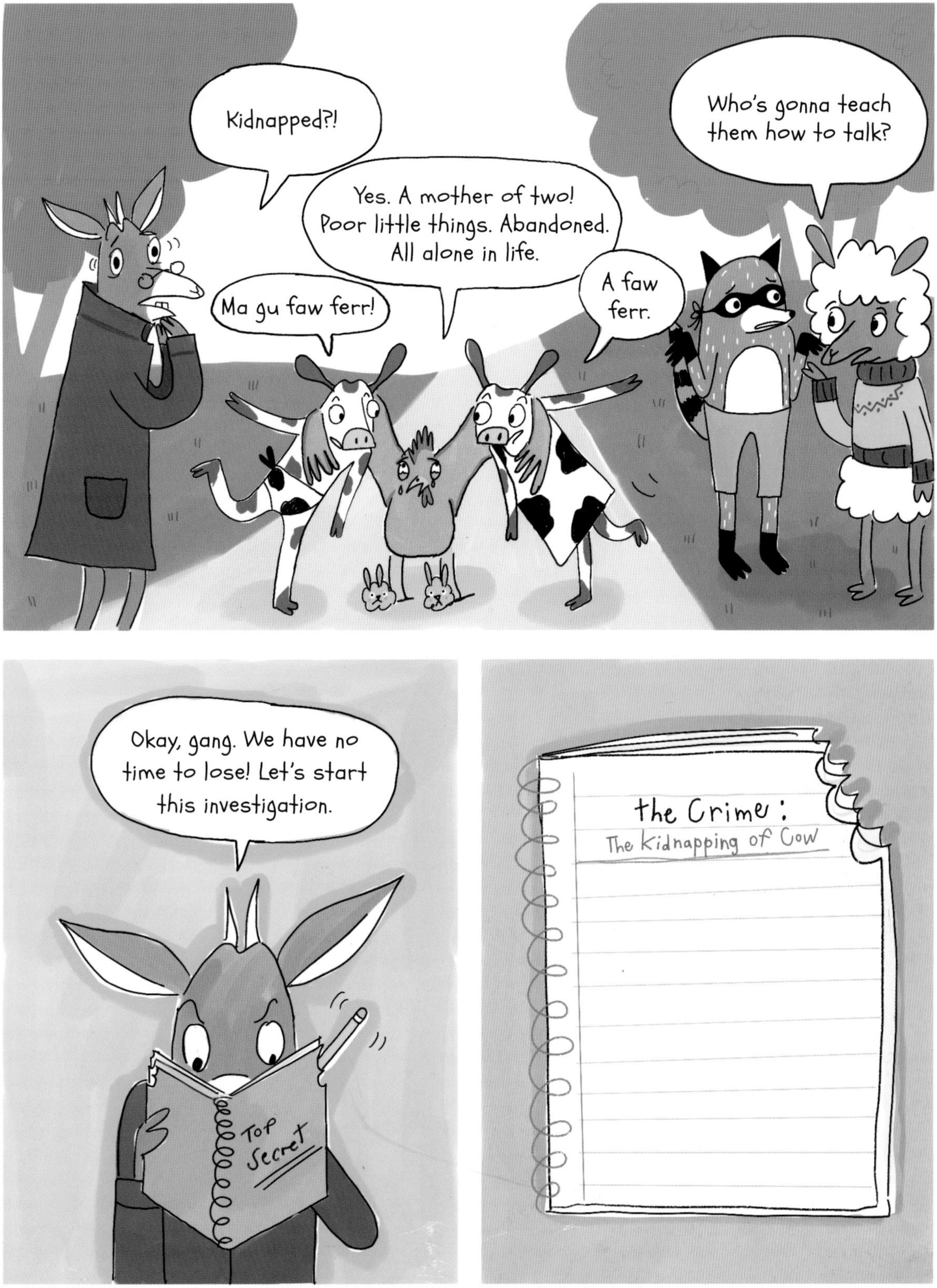
Kidnapped?!
Yes. A mother of two! Poor little things. Abandoned. All alone in life.
Ma gu faw ferr!
A faw ferr.
Who's gonna teach them how to talk?
Okay, gang. We have no time to lose! Let's start this investigation.
Top Secret
the Crime:
The Kidnapping of Cow

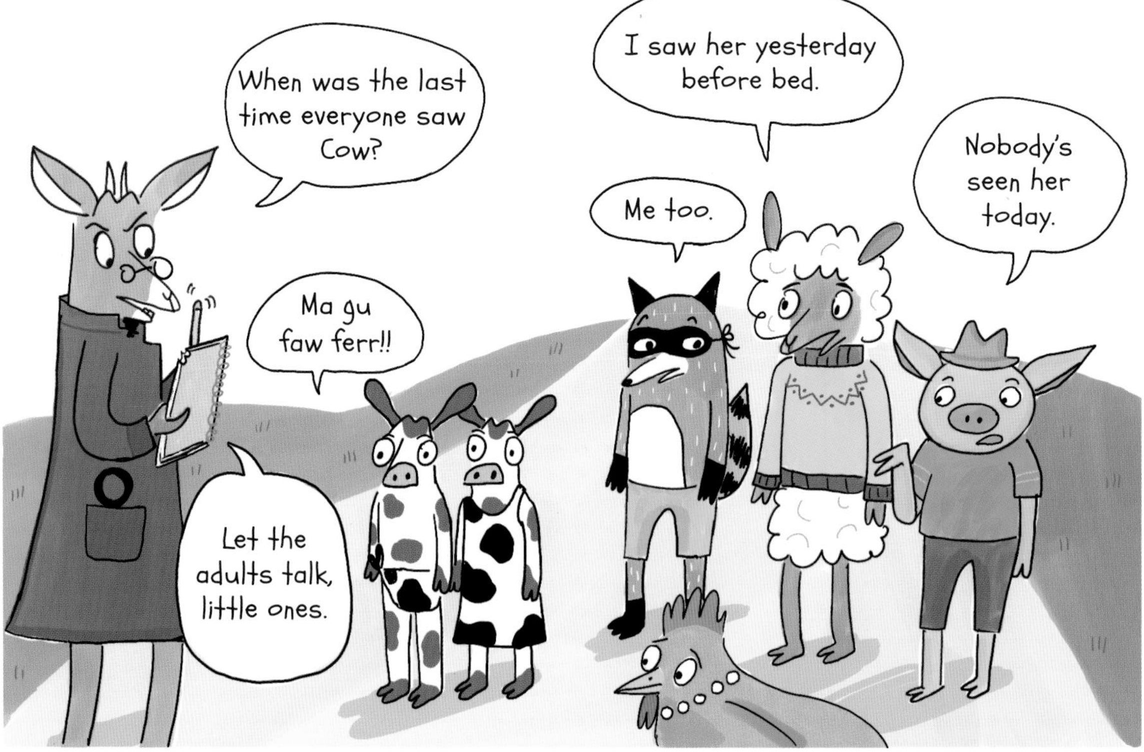
When was the last time everyone saw Cow?
Ma gu faw ferr!!
Let the adults talk, little ones.
I saw her yesterday before bed.
Me too.
Nobody's seen her today.

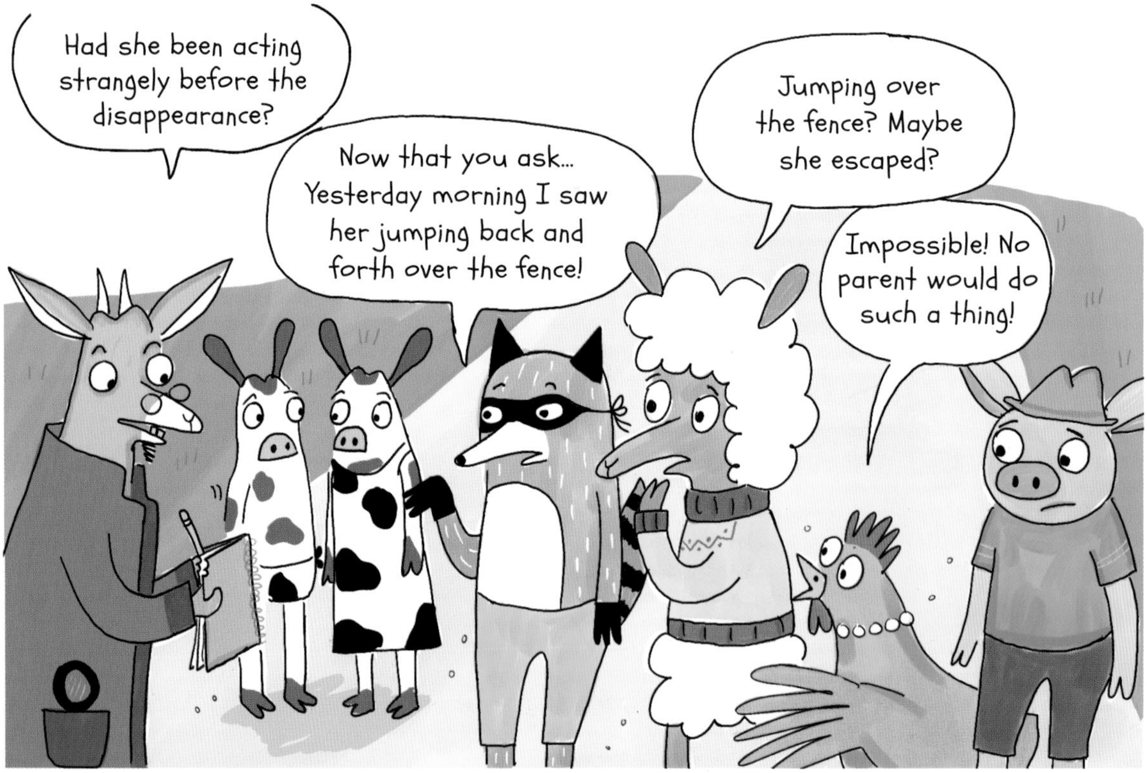
Had she been acting strangely before the disappearance?
Now that you ask... Yesterday morning I saw her jumping back and forth over the fence!
Jumping over the fence? Maybe she escaped?
Impossible! No parent would do such a thing!

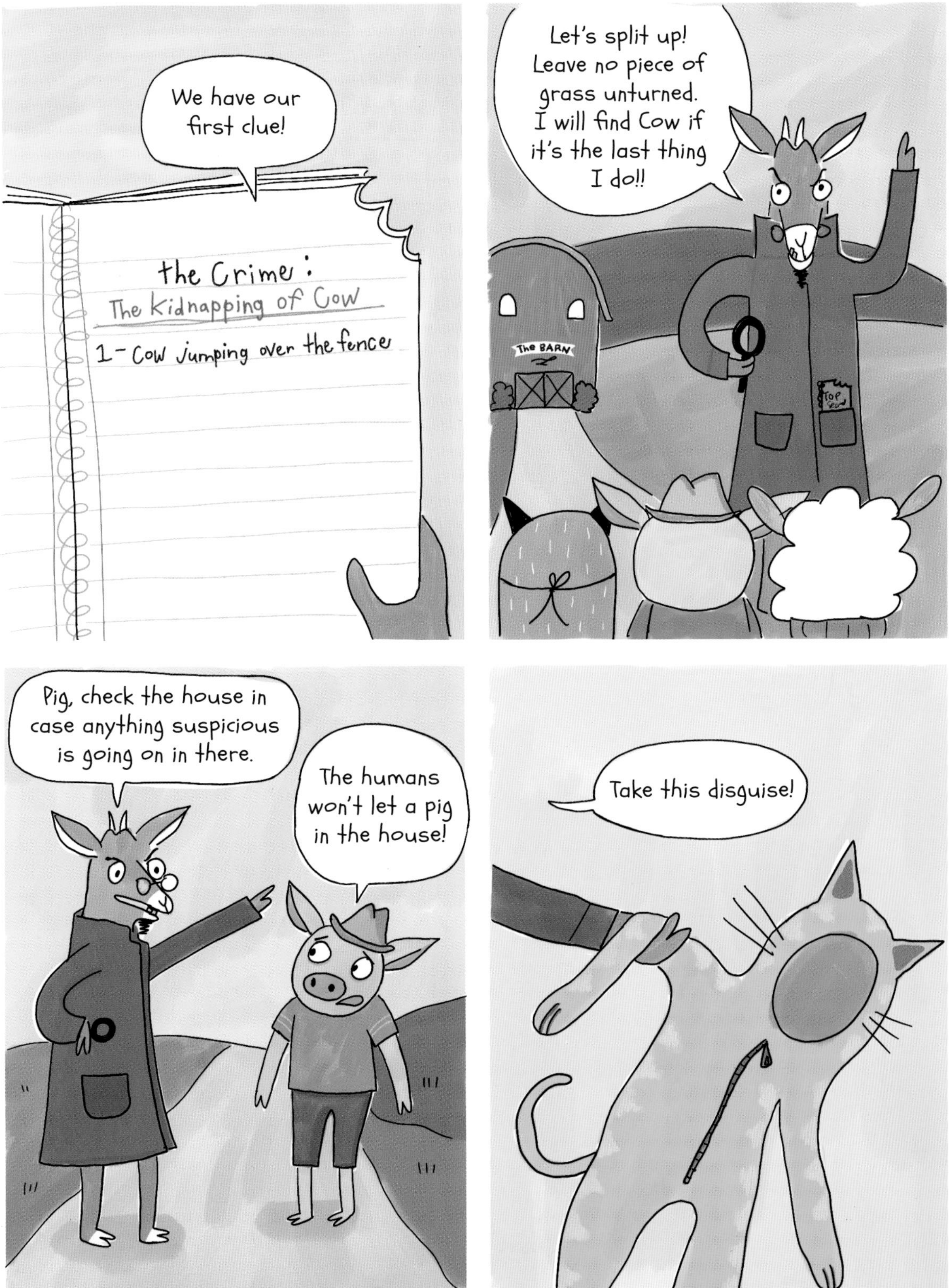
We have our first clue!
the Crime:
The Kidnapping of Cow
1- Cow jumping over the fence
Let's split up! Leave no piece of grass unturned. I will find Cow if it's the last thing I do!!
The BARN
Pig, check the house in case anything suspicious is going on in there.
The humans won't let a pig in the house!
Take this disguise!

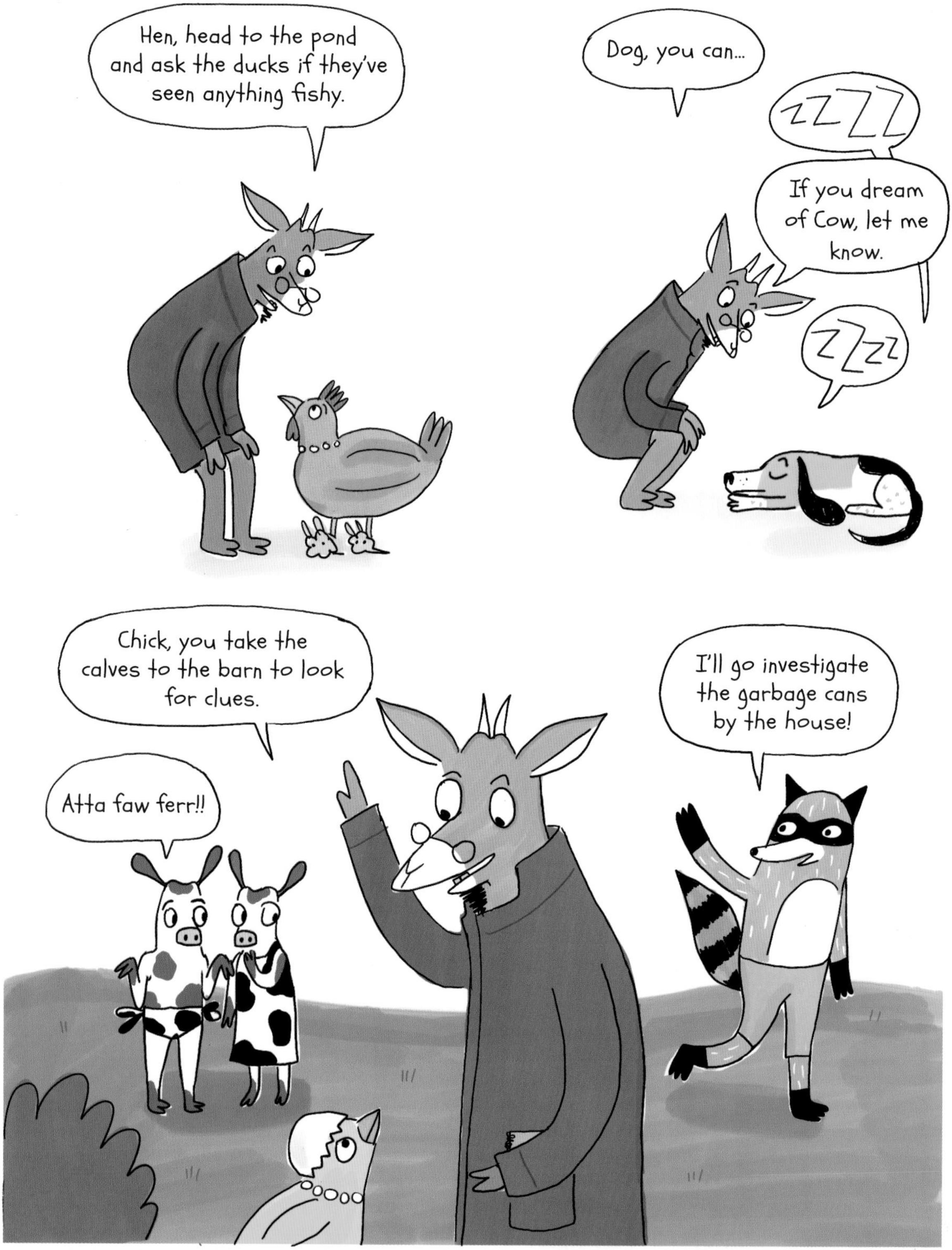
Hen, head to the pond and ask the ducks if they've seen anything fishy.
Dog, you can...
ZZZZ
If you dream of Cow, let me know.
ZZZZ
Chick, you take the calves to the barn to look for clues.
I'll go investigate the garbage cans by the house!
Atta faw ferr!!

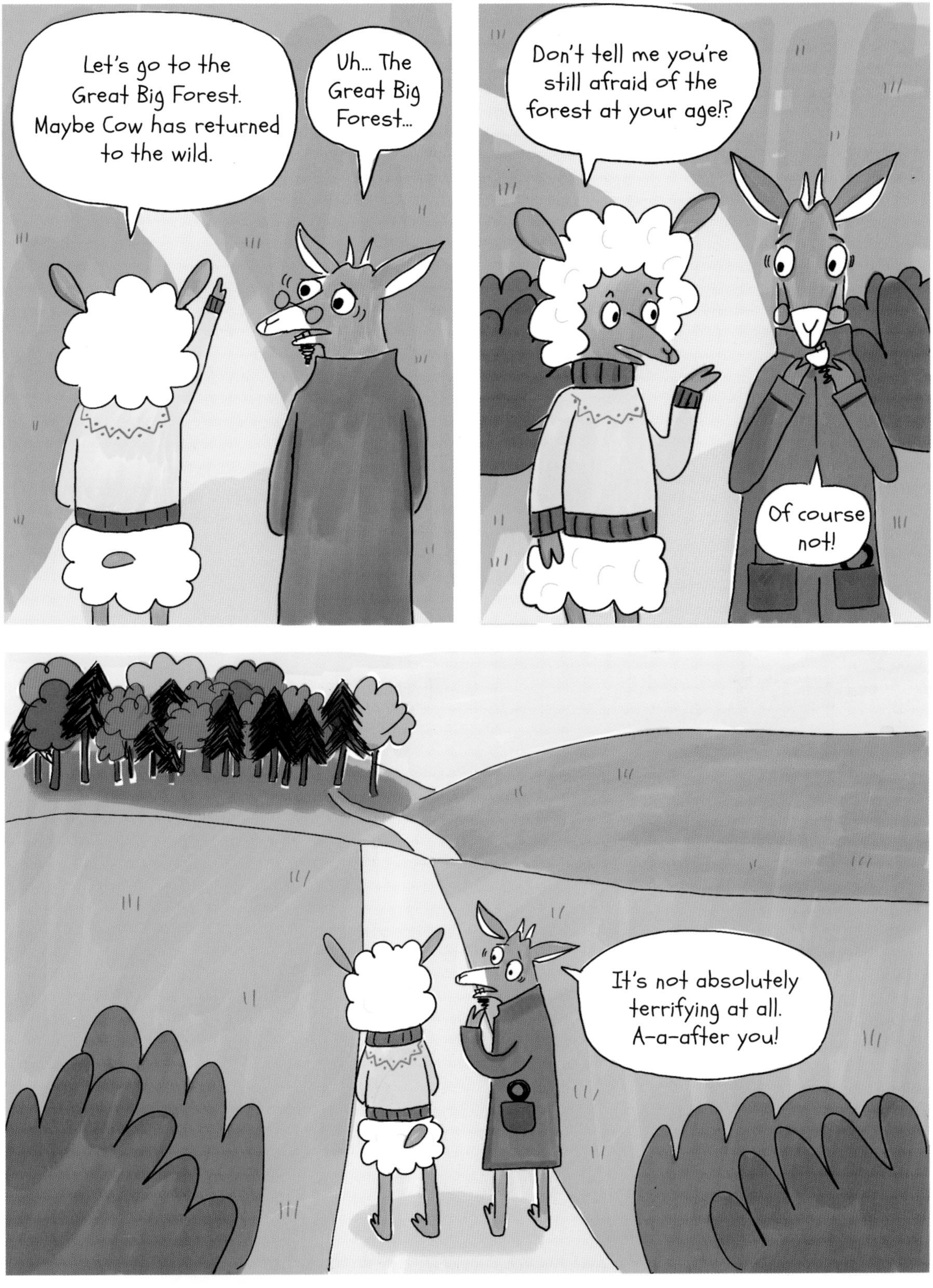
Let's go to the Great Big Forest. Maybe Cow has returned to the wild.
Uh... The Great Big Forest...
Don't tell me you're still afraid of the forest at your age!?
Of course not!
It's not absolutely terrifying at all. A-a-after you!

On their way to the Great Big Forest, they came across something very strange in the cornfield.

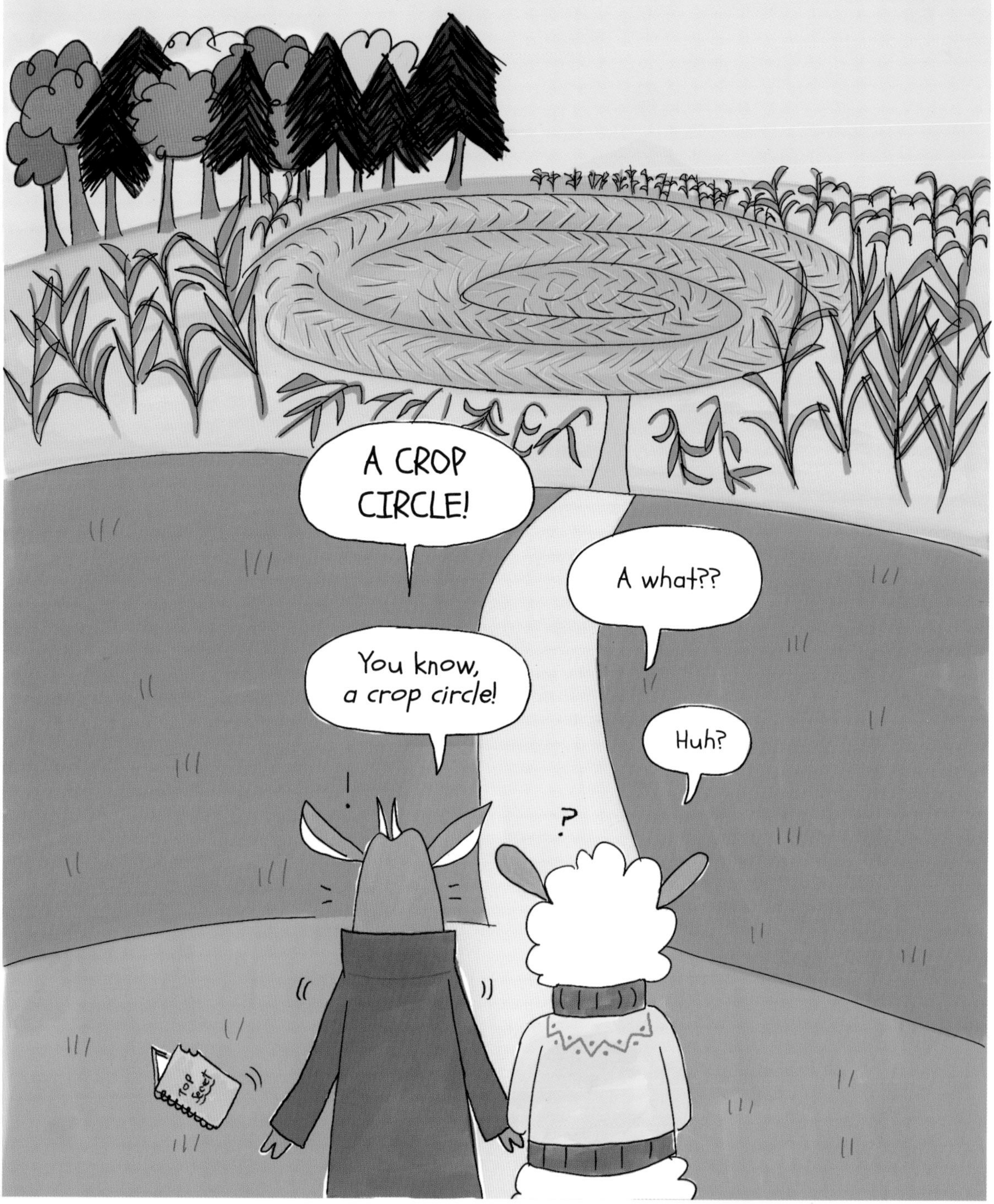
A CROP CIRCLE!
A what??
You know, a crop circle!
Huh?
TOP Secret

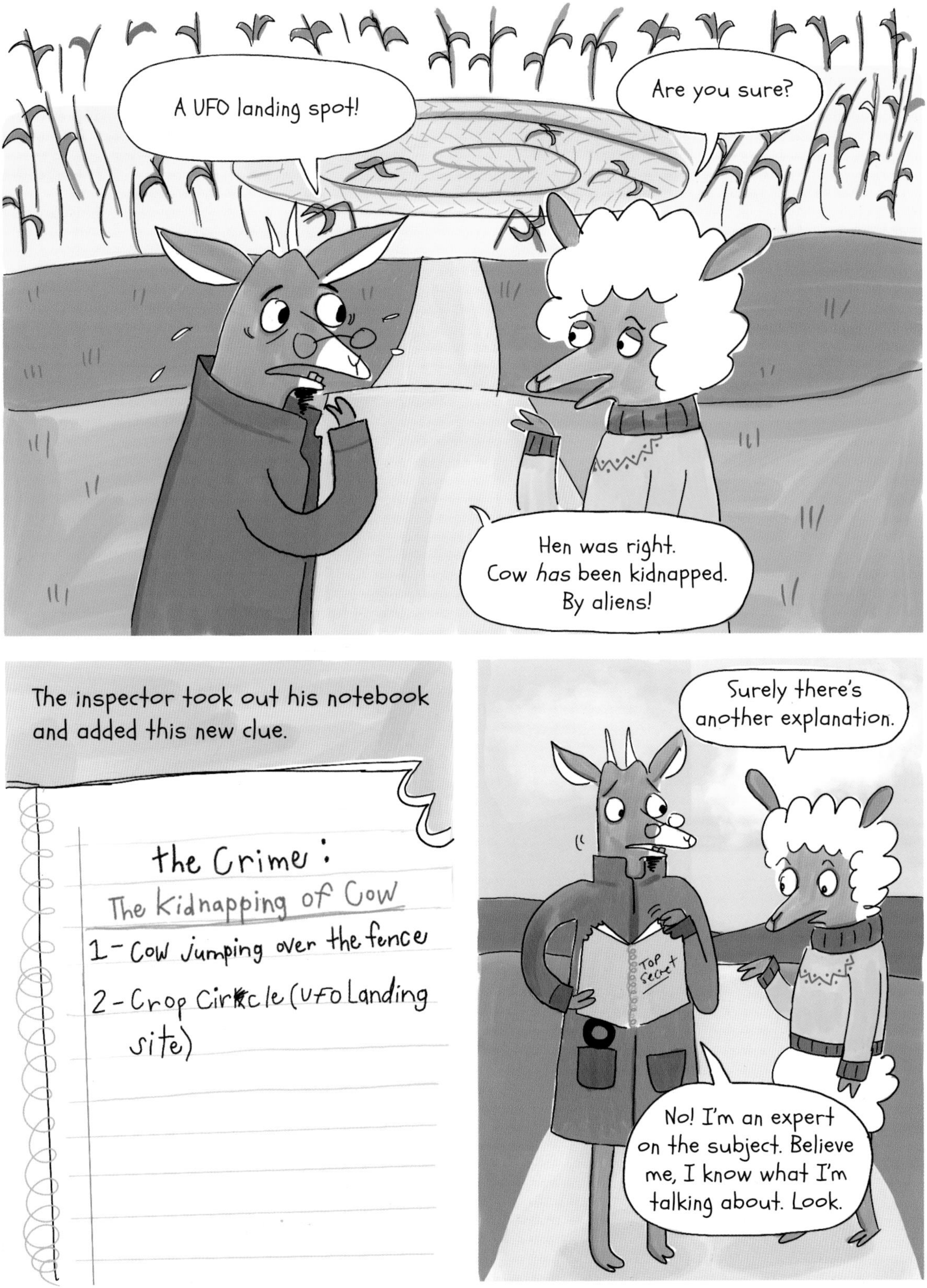
A UFO landing spot!
Are you sure?
Hen was right. Cow *has* been kidnapped. By aliens!
The inspector took out his notebook and added this new clue.
the Crime:
The Kidnapping of Cow
1- Cow Jumping over the fence
2- Crop Cirkcle (UFO Landing site)
Surely there's another explanation.
TOP secret
No! I'm an expert on the subject. Believe me, I know what I'm talking about. Look.

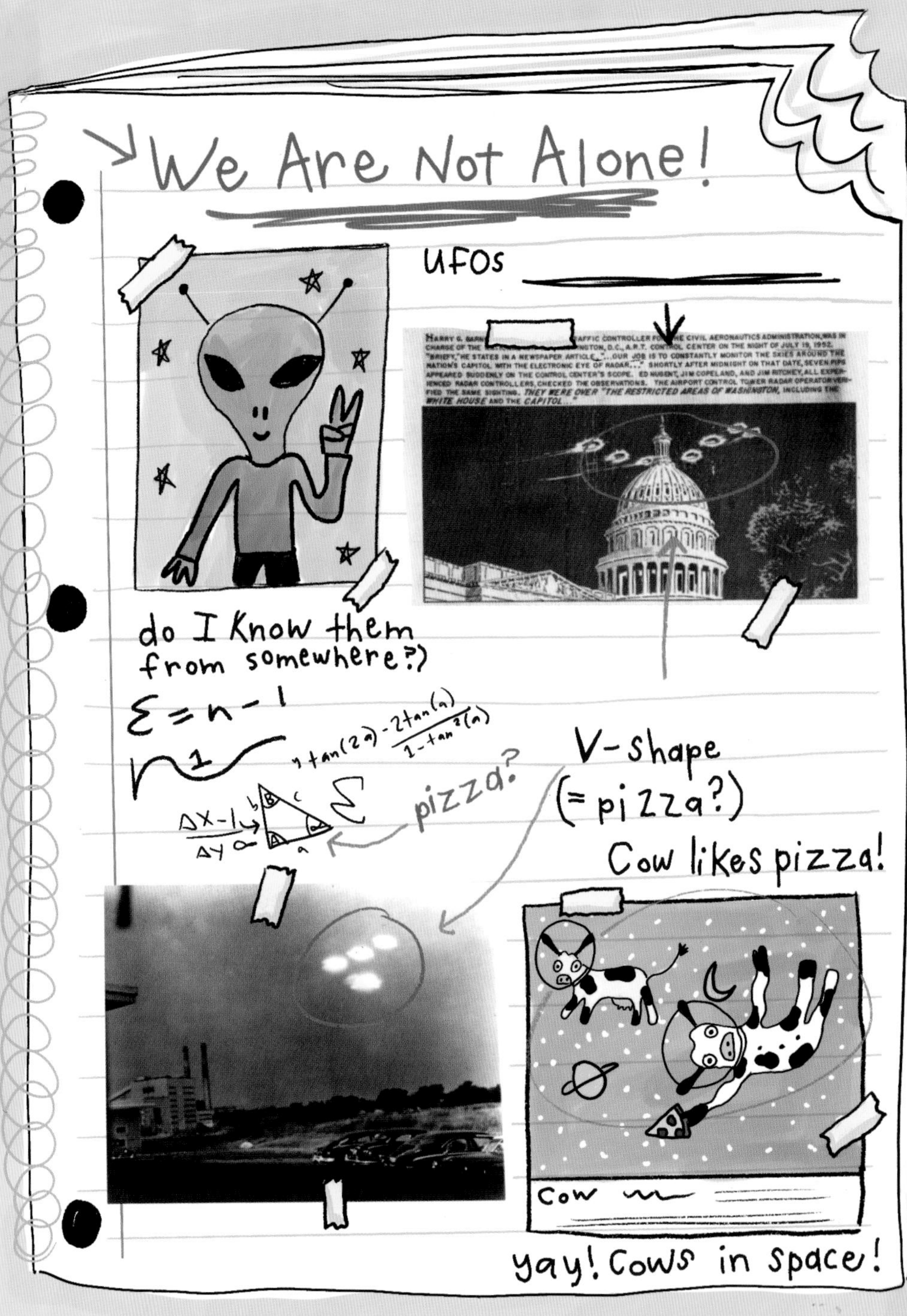
We Are Not Alone!
UFOs
HARRY G. BARN
AFFIC CONTROLLER FO
HE CIVIL AERONAUTICS ADMINISTRATION, WAS IN CHARGE OF THE
NGTON, D.C., A.R.T. CONTROL CENTER ON THE NIGHT OF JULY 19, 1952.
"BRIEFLY," HE STATES IN A NEWSPAPER ARTICLE, "...OUR JOB IS TO CONSTANTLY MONITOR THE SKIES AROUND THE NATION'S CAPITOL WITH THE ELECTRONIC EYE OF RADAR..." SHORTLY AFTER MIDNIGHT ON THAT DATE, SEVEN PIPS APPEARED SUDDENLY ON THE CONTROL CENTER'S SCOPE. ED NUGENT, JIM COPELAND, AND JIM RITCHEY, ALL EXPERIENCED RADAR CONTROLLERS, CHECKED THE OBSERVATIONS. THE AIRPORT CONTROL TOWER RADAR OPERATOR VERIFIED THE SAME SIGHTING. THEY WERE OVER "THE RESTRICTED AREAS OF WASHINGTON, INCLUDING THE WHITE HOUSE AND THE CAPITOL..."
do I Know them from somewhere?)
Σ = n - 1
pizza?
V-shape (= pizza?)
Cow likes pizza!
Cow
yay! Cows in space!

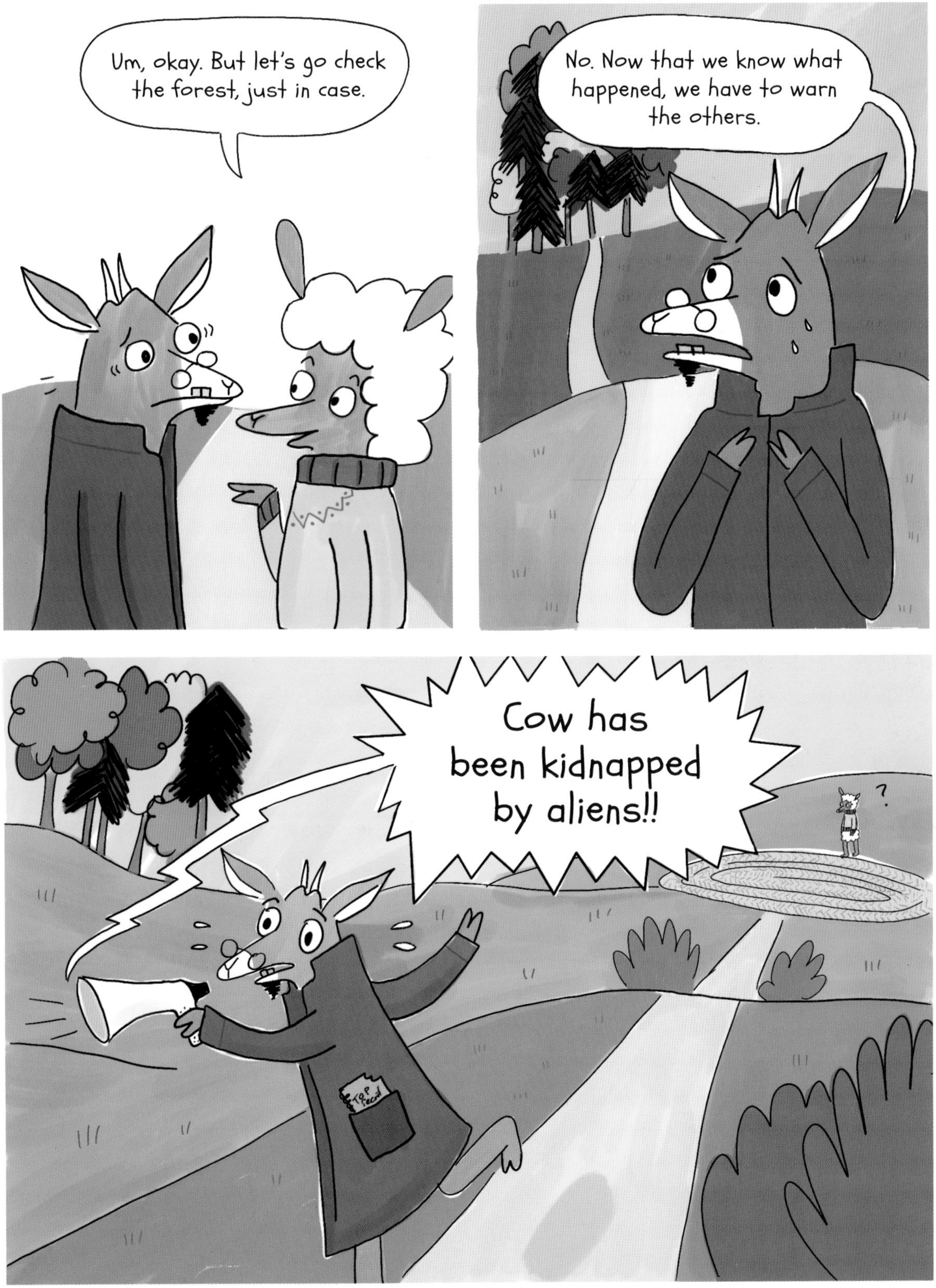
Um, okay. But let's go check the forest, just in case.
No. Now that we know what happened, we have to warn the others.
Cow has been kidnapped by aliens!!
?

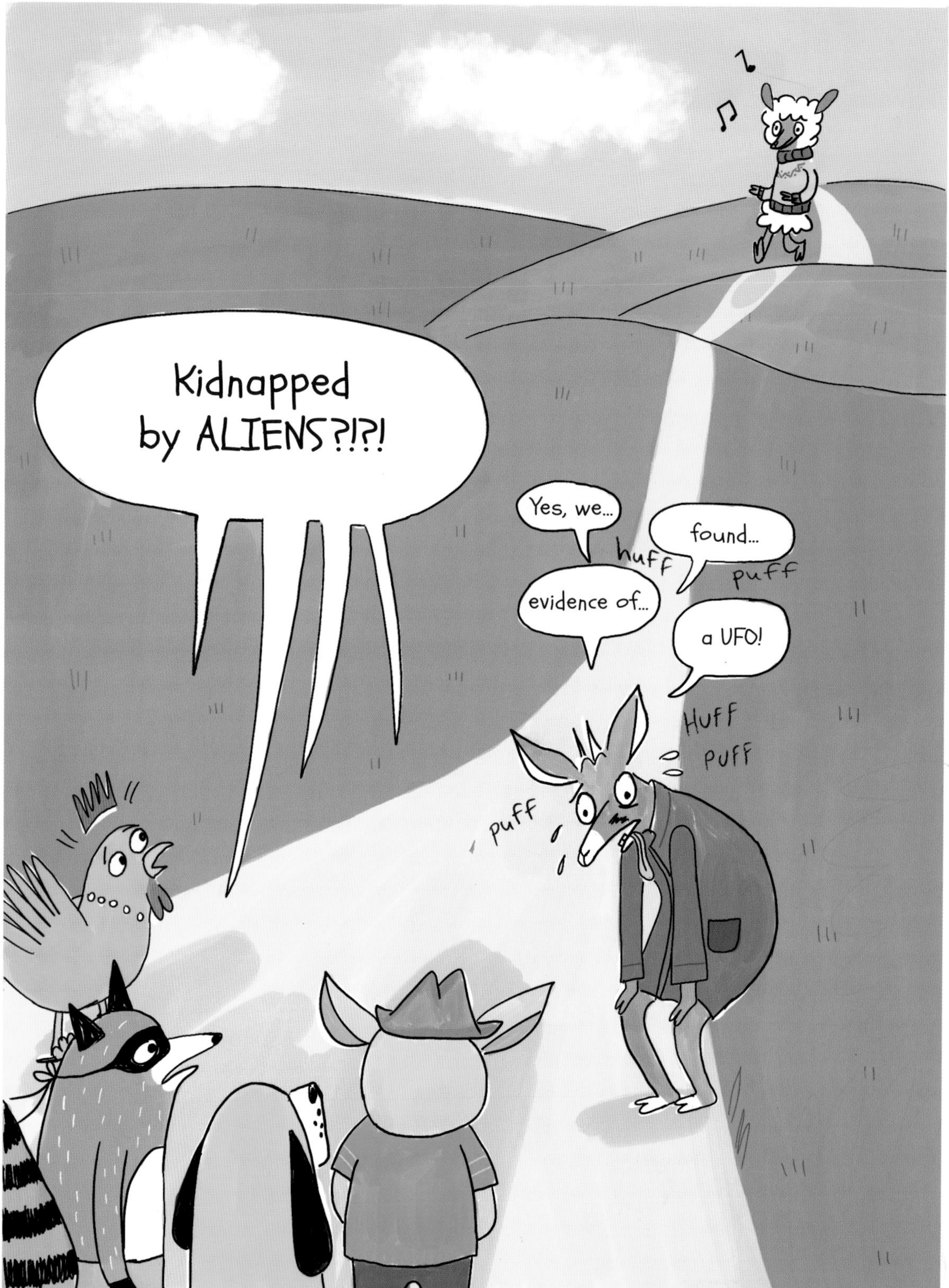
Kidnapped by ALIENS?!?!
Yes, we...
huff
found...
puff
evidence of...
a UFO!
HUFF
PUFF
puff

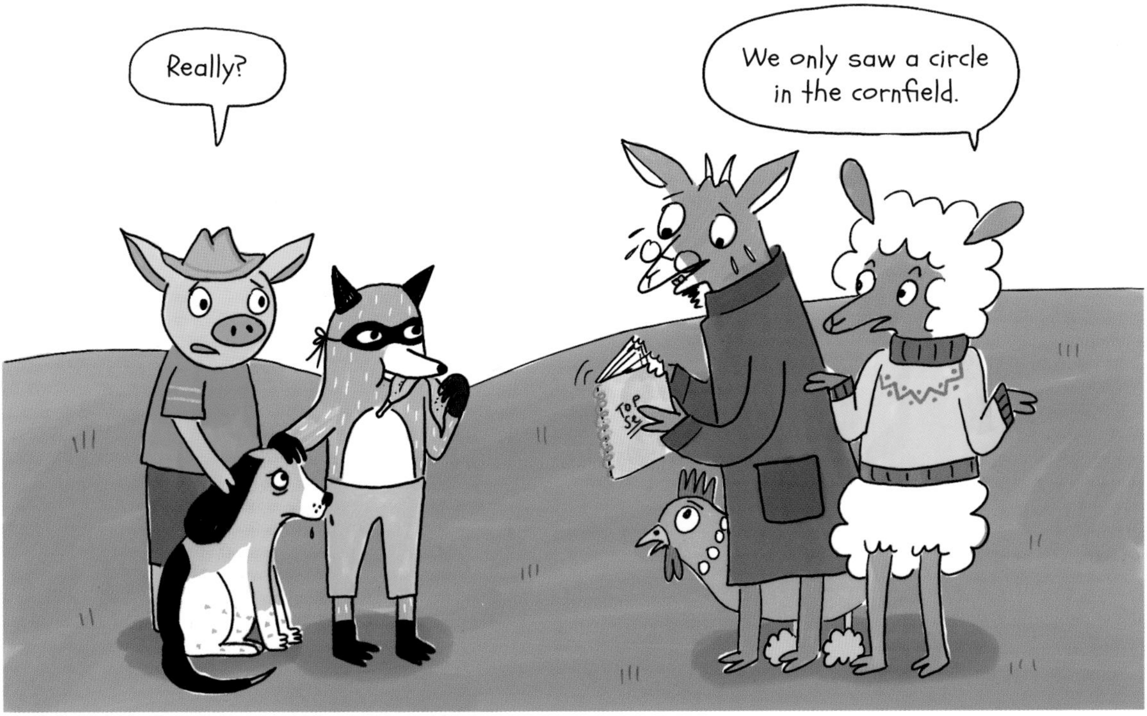
Really?
We only saw a circle in the cornfield.
TOP SE

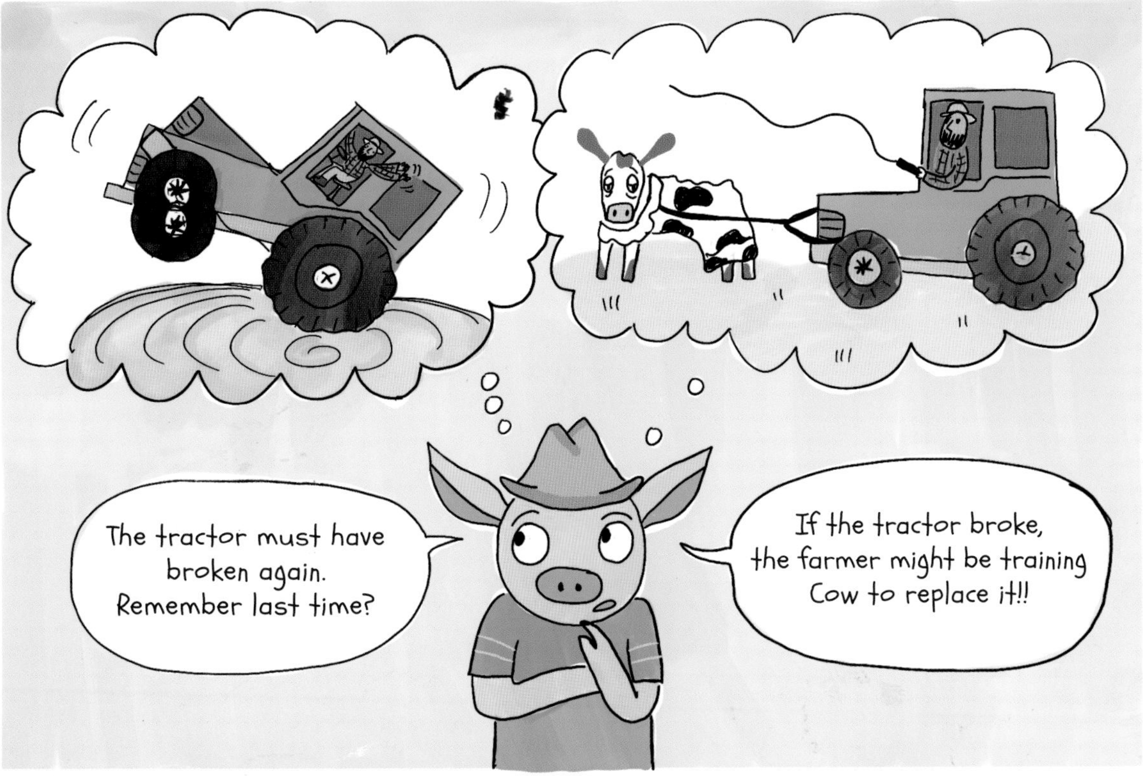
The tractor must have broken again. Remember last time?
If the tractor broke, the farmer might be training Cow to replace it!!

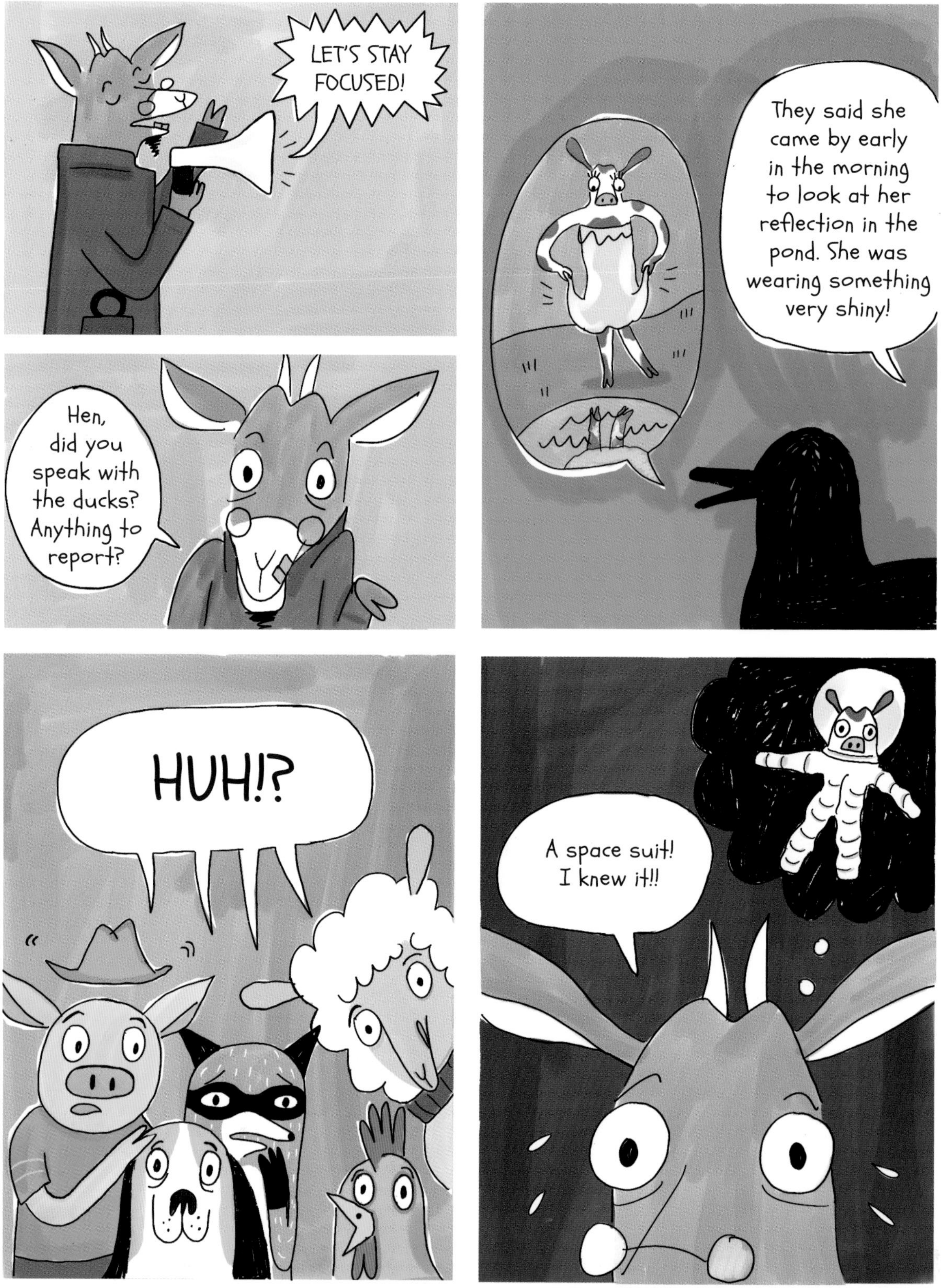
LET'S STAY FOCUSED!
Hen, did you speak with the ducks? Anything to report?
They said she came by early in the morning to look at her reflection in the pond. She was wearing something very shiny!
HUH!?
A space suit! I knew it!!

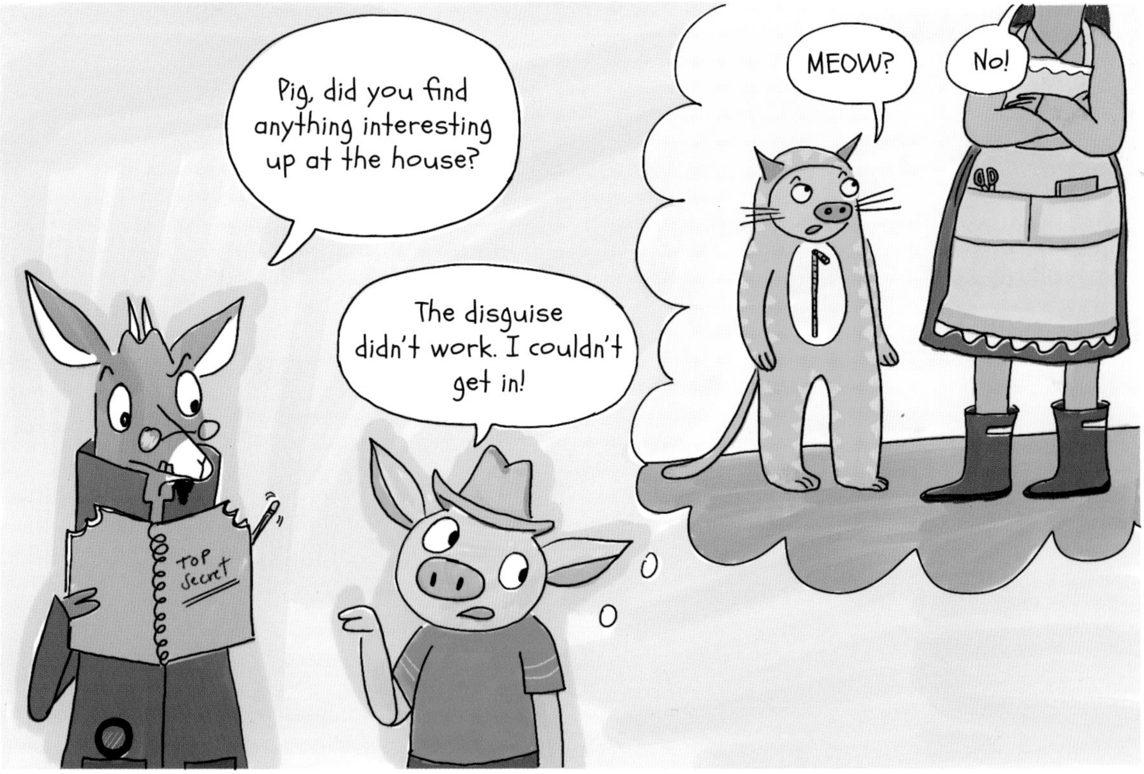
Pig, did you find anything interesting up at the house?
The disguise didn't work. I couldn't get in!
MEOW?
No!
TOP Secret

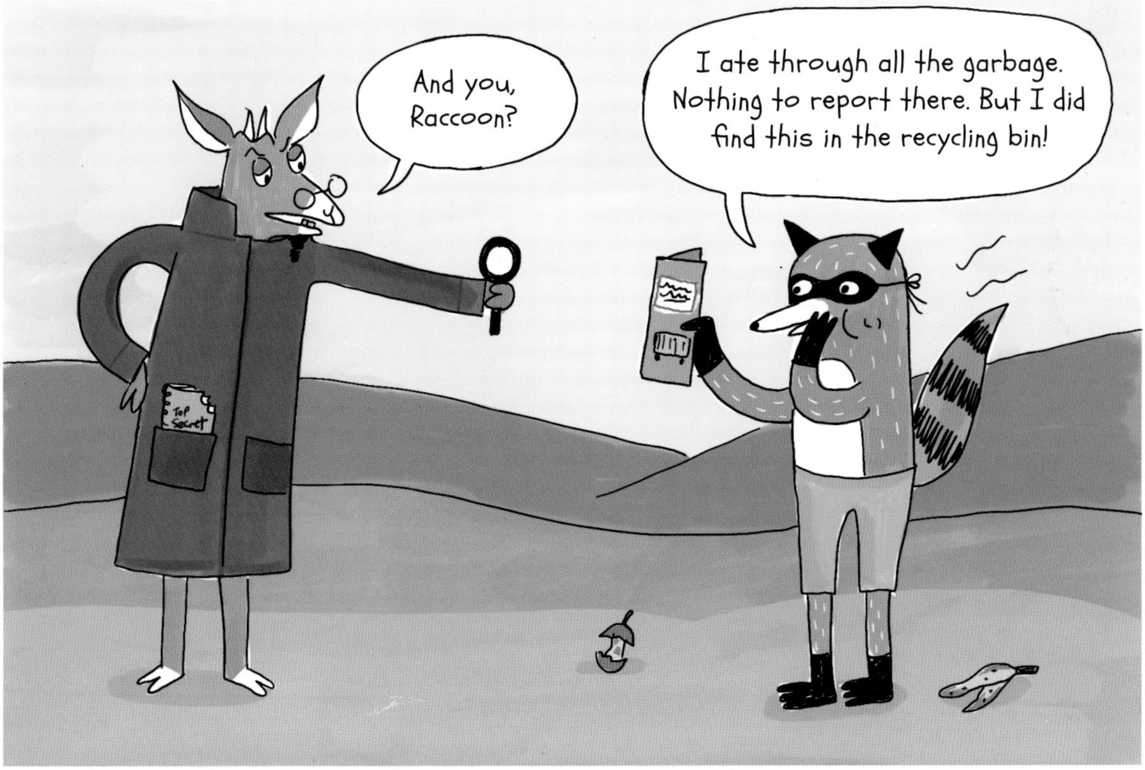
And you, Raccoon?
I ate through all the garbage. Nothing to report there. But I did find this in the recycling bin!
TOP Secret

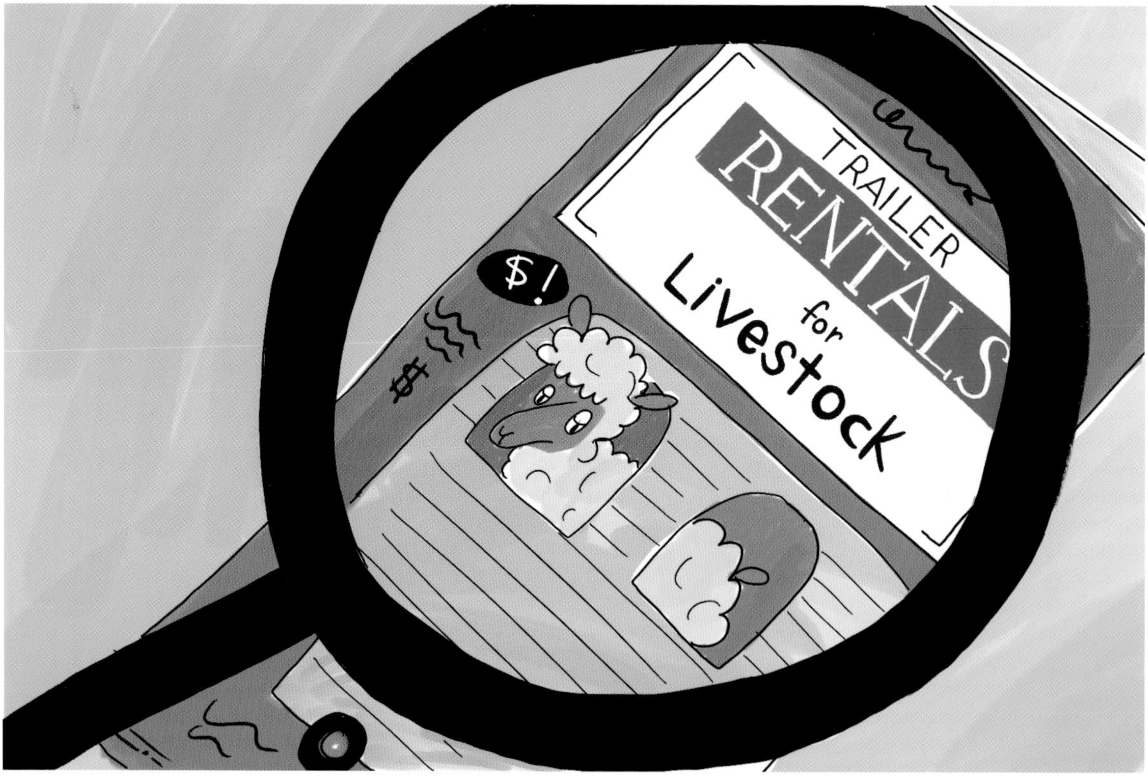
TRAILER
RENTALS
for
Livestock
$!

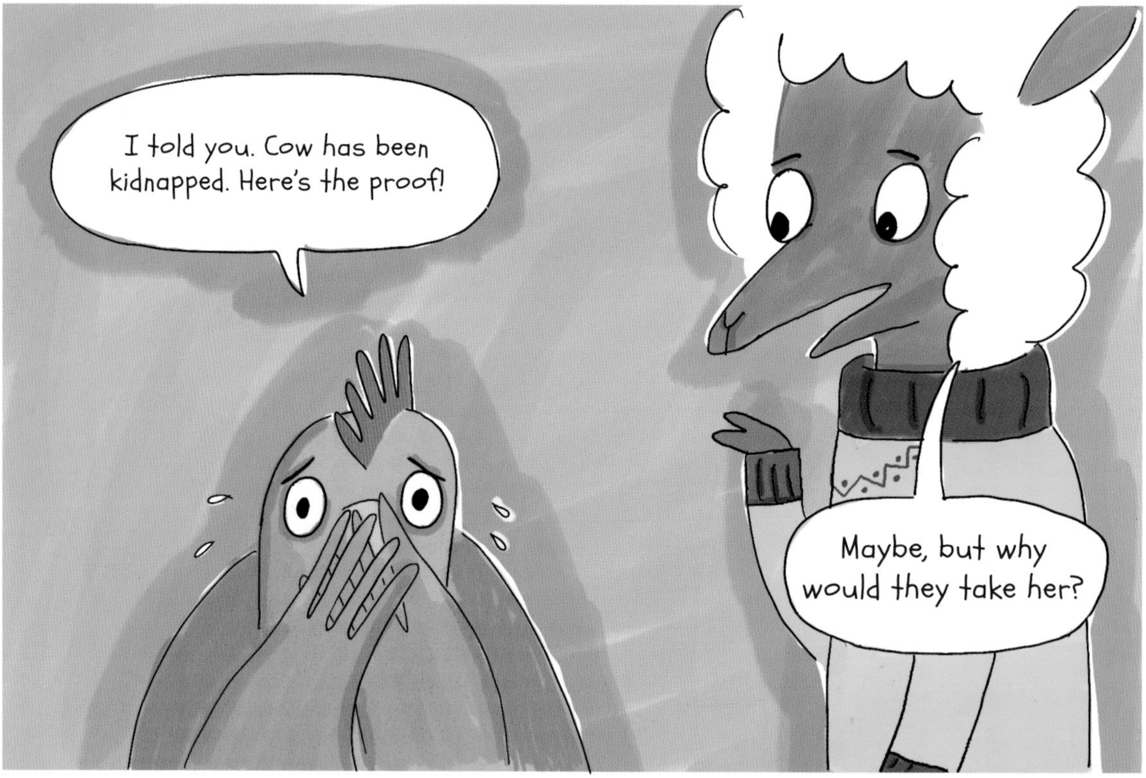
I told you. Cow has been kidnapped. Here's the proof!
Maybe, but why would they take her?

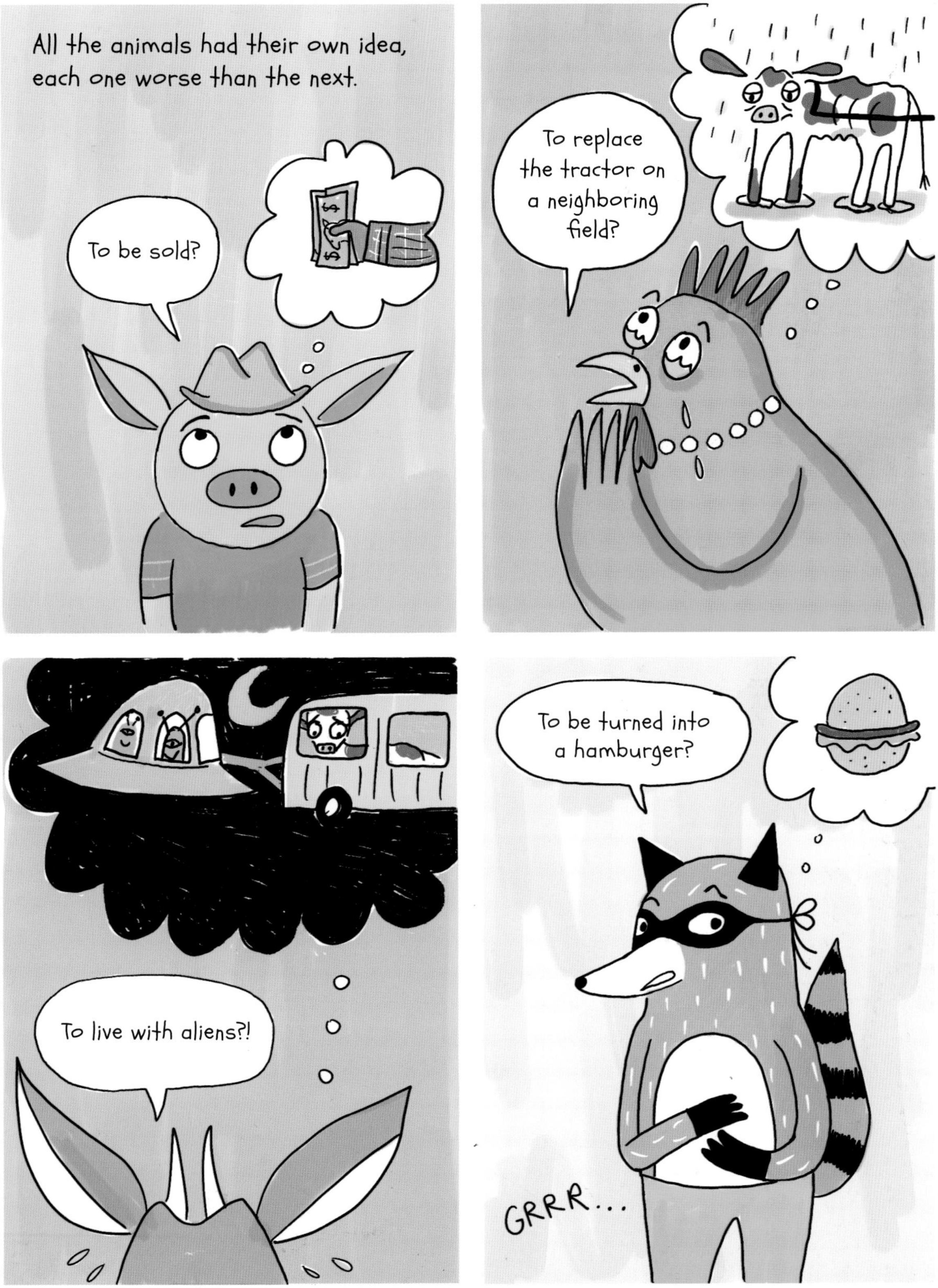
All the animals had their own idea, each one worse than the next.
To be sold?
To replace the tractor on a neighboring field?
To live with aliens?!
To be turned into a hamburger?
GRRR...

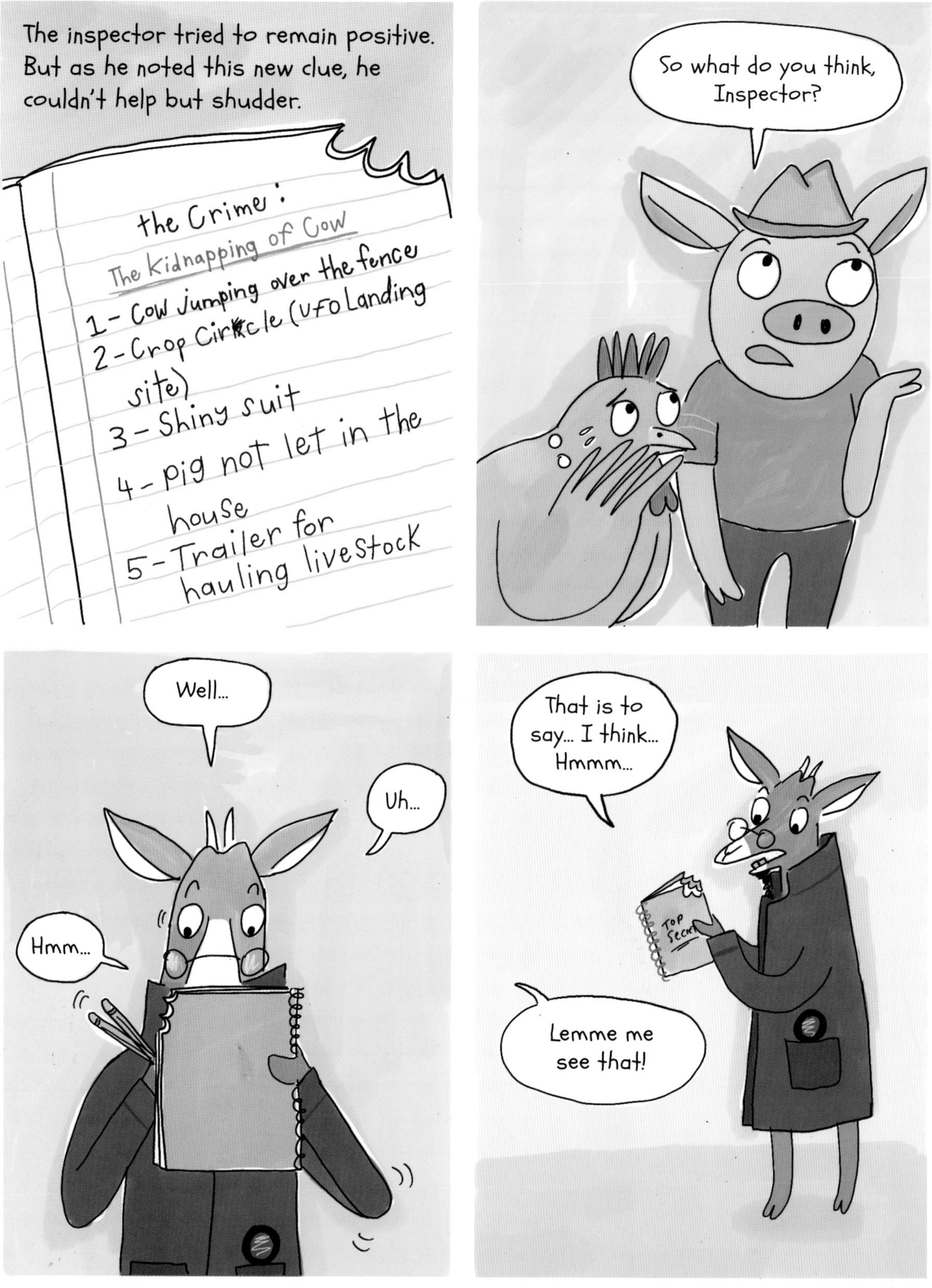

The inspector tried to remain positive. But as he noted this new clue, he couldn't help but shudder.
the Crime:
The Kidnapping of Cow
1- Cow jumping over the fence
2- Crop Cir~~k~~cle (UFO Landing site)
3- Shiny suit
4- pig not let in the house
5- Trailer for hauling livestock
So what do you think, Inspector?
Well...
Uh...
Hmm...
That is to say... I think... Hmmm...
Top Secret
Lemme me see that!

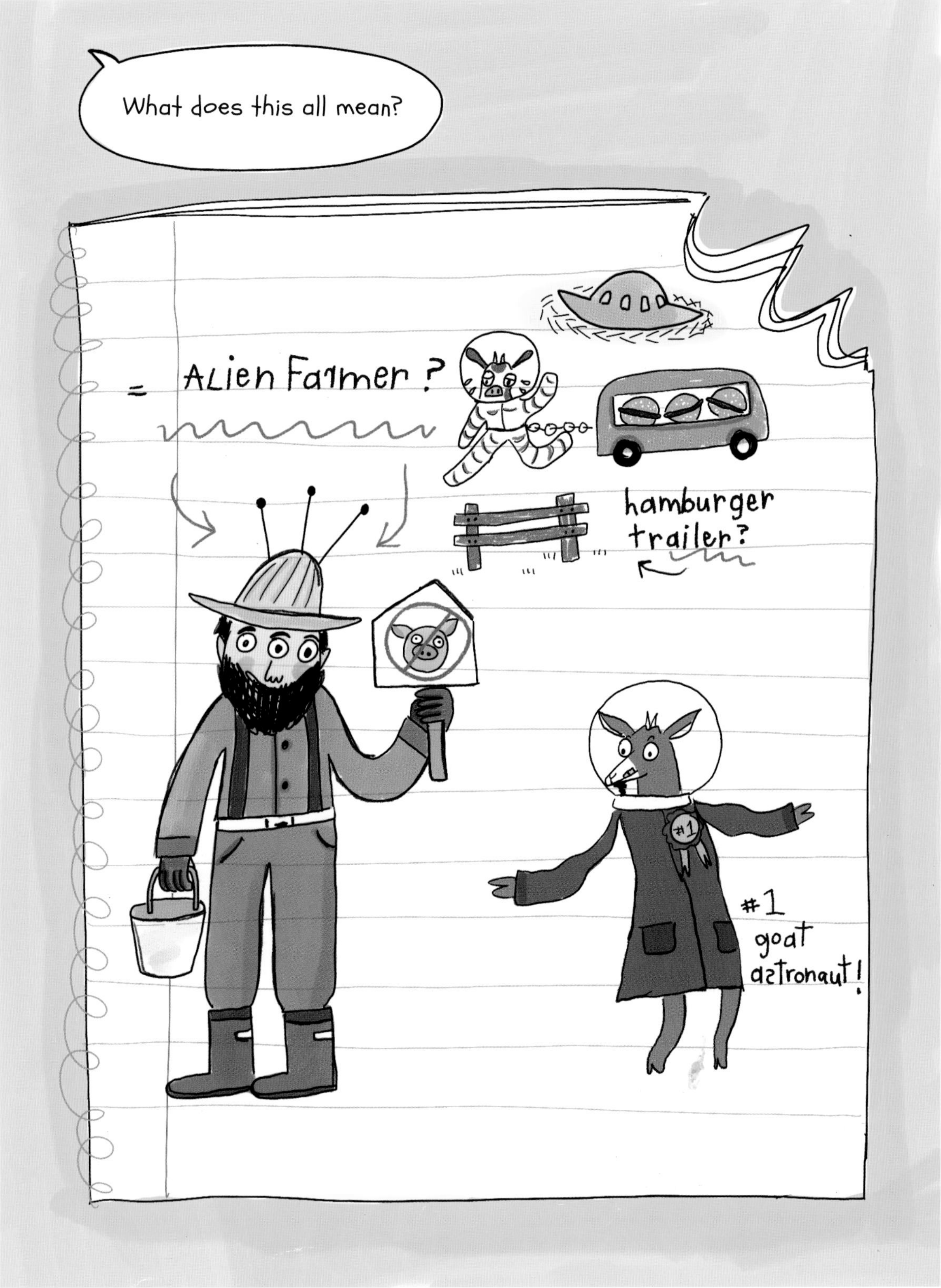
What does this all mean?
= Alien Farmer ?
hamburger trailer?
#1 goat astronaut!

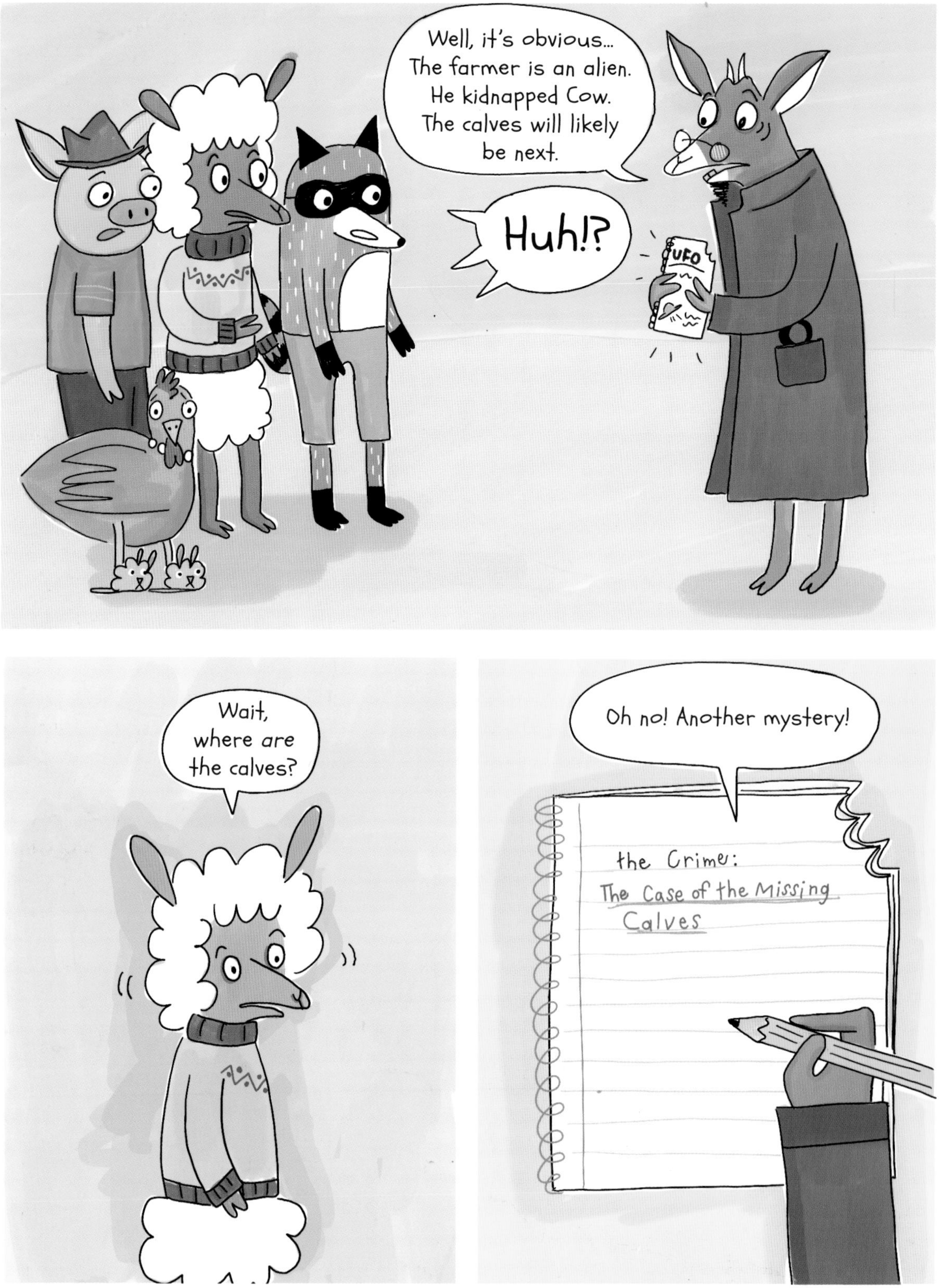
Well, it's obvious... The farmer is an alien. He kidnapped Cow. The calves will likely be next.
Huh!?
UFO
Wait, where *are* the calves?
Oh no! Another mystery!
the Crime:
The Case of the Missing Calves

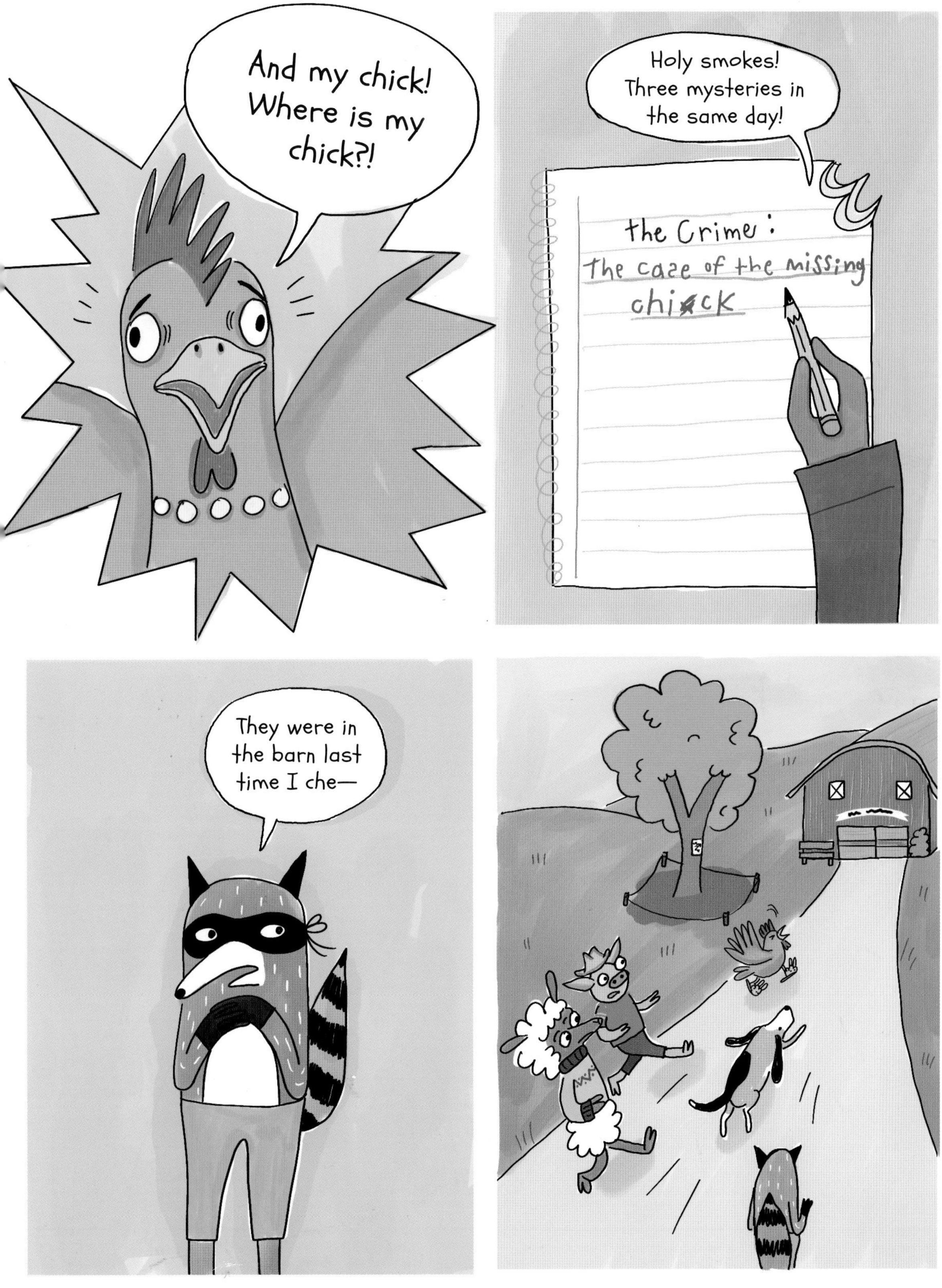
And my chick! Where is my chick?!
Holy smokes! Three mysteries in the same day!
the Crime:
The caze of the missing chick
They were in the barn last time I che—

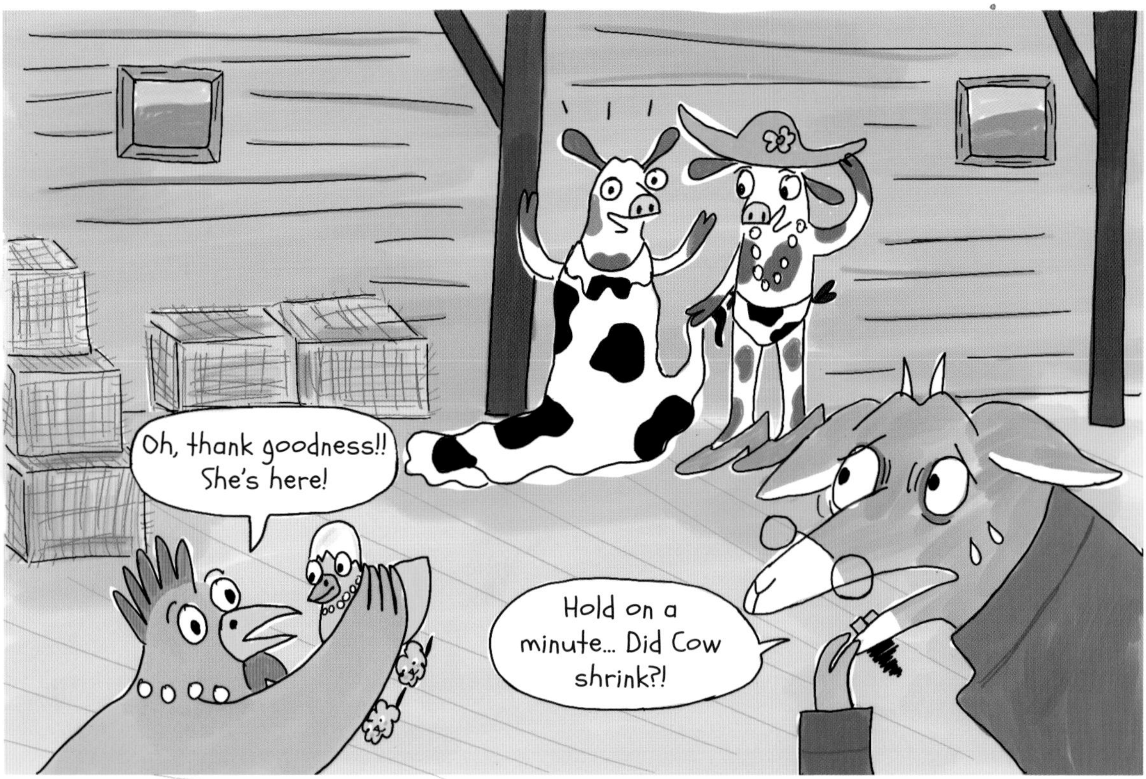
Oh, thank goodness!! She's here!
Hold on a minute... Did Cow shrink?!

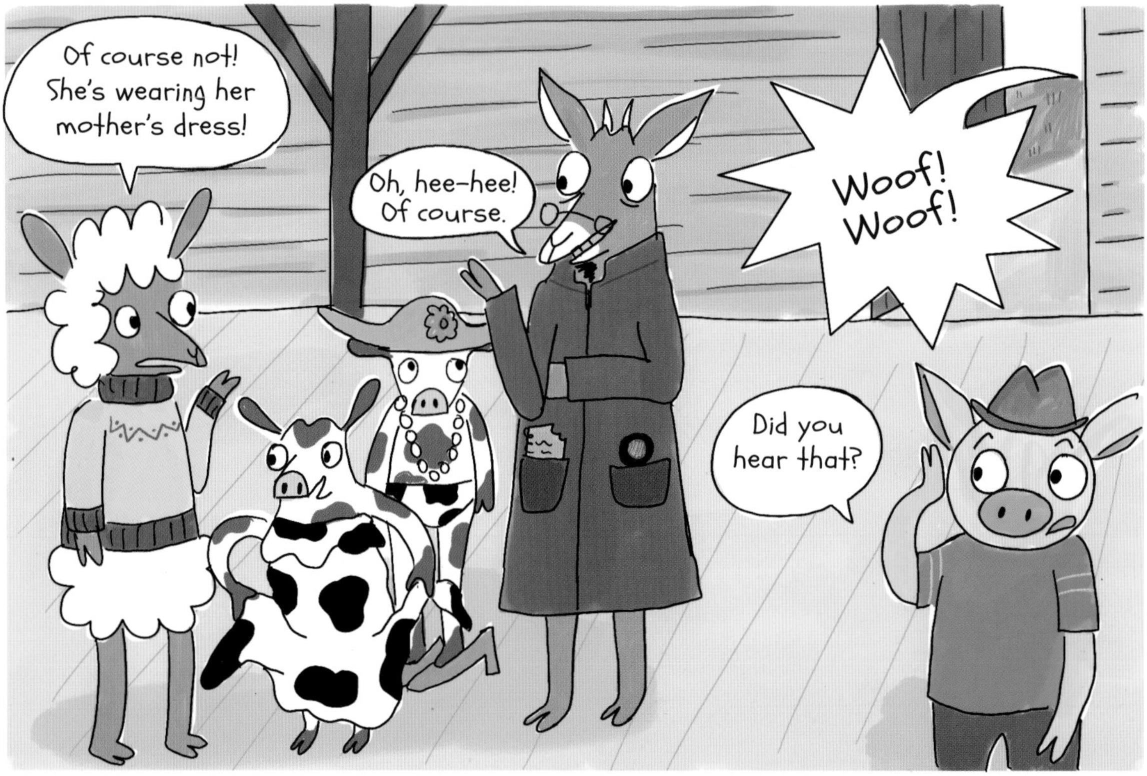
Of course not! She's wearing her mother's dress!
Oh, hee-hee! Of course.
Woof! Woof!
Did you hear that?

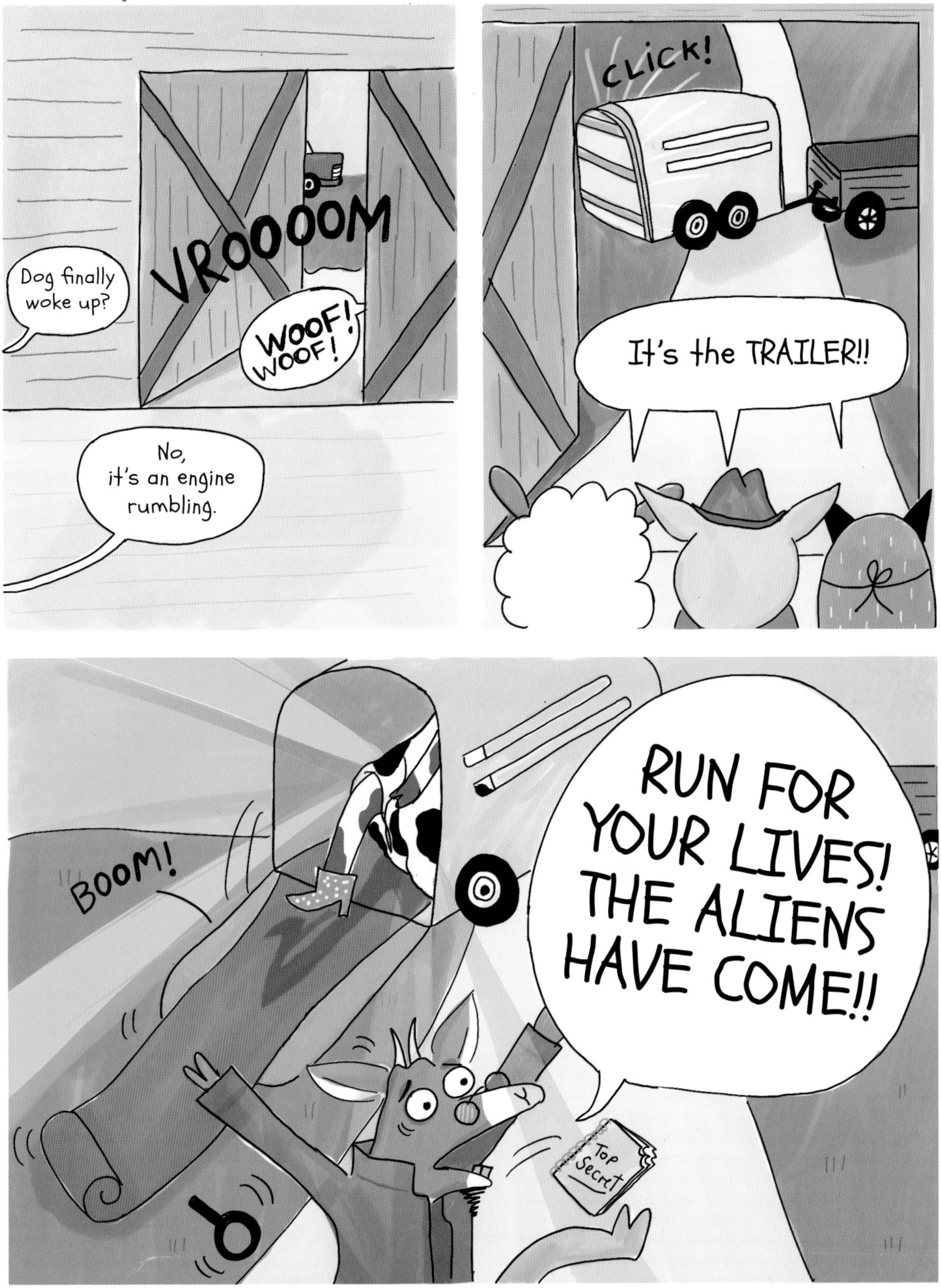
VROOOOM
Dog finally woke up?
WOOF! WOOF!
No, it's an engine rumbling.
CLICK!
It's the TRAILER!!
BOOM!
RUN FOR YOUR LIVES! THE ALIENS HAVE COME!!
Top Secret

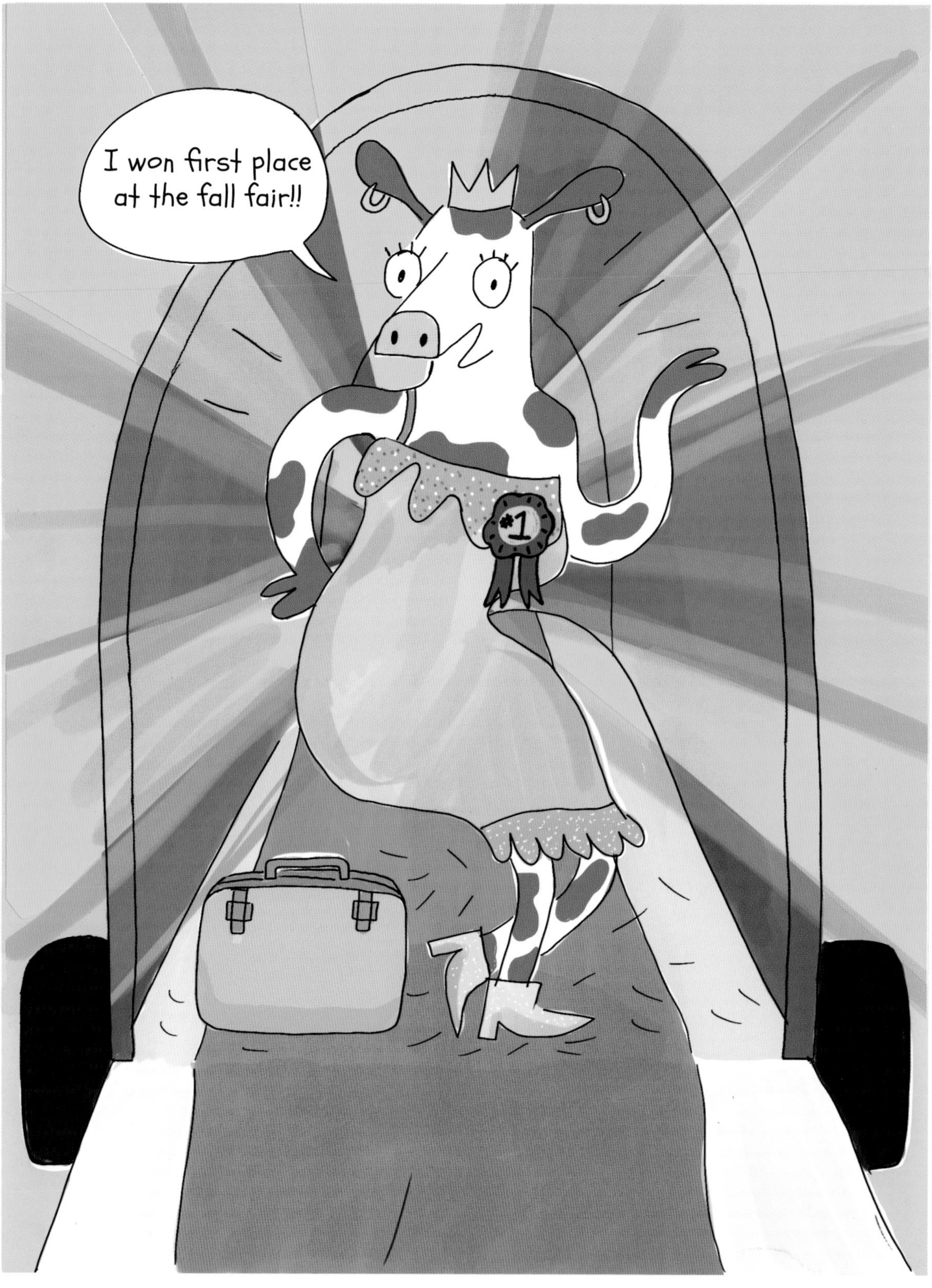
I won first place at the fall fair!!
#1

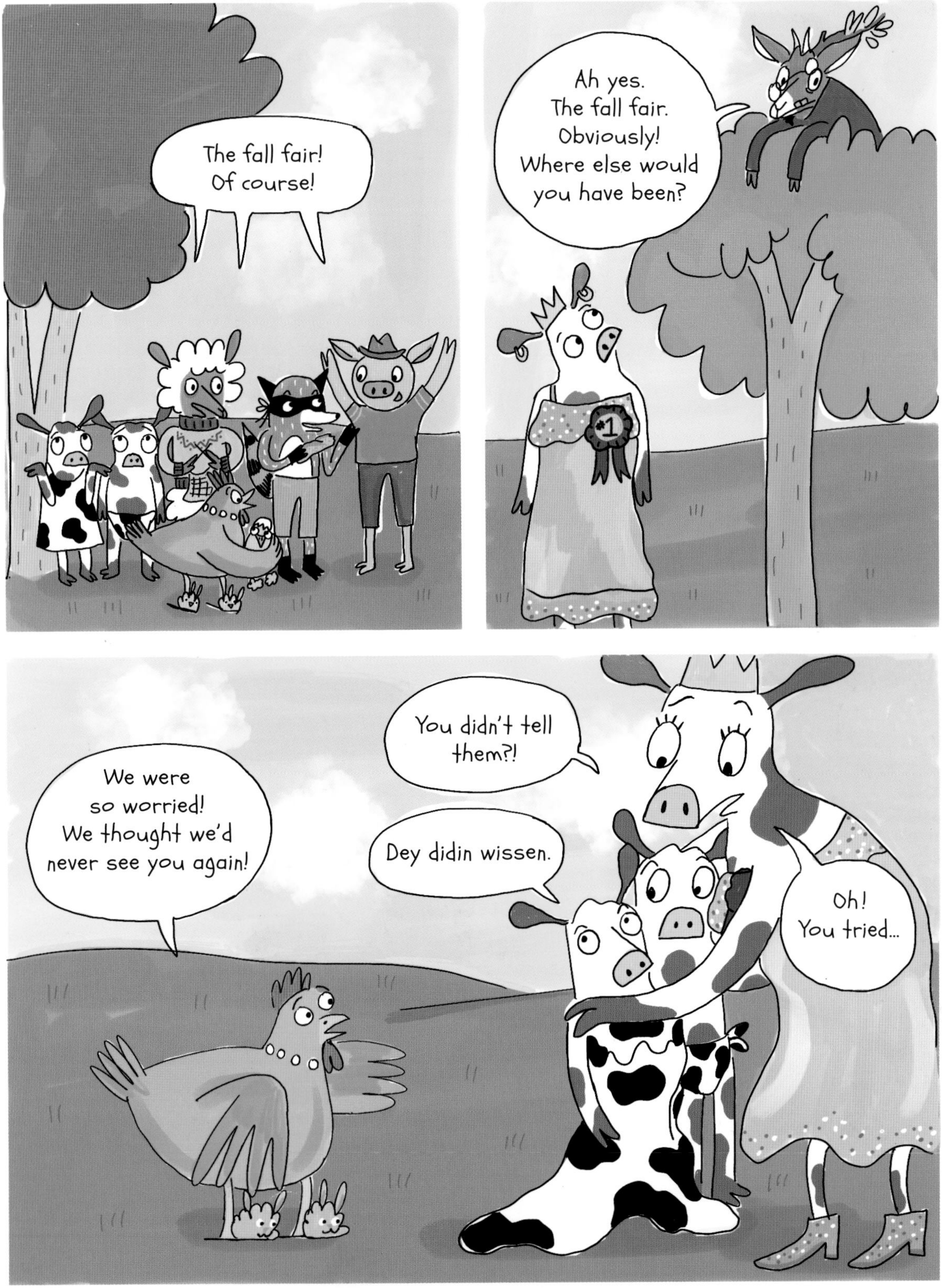
The fall fair! Of course!
Ah yes. The fall fair. Obviously! Where else would you have been?
We were so worried! We thought we'd never see you again!
You didn't tell them?!
Dey didin wissen.
Oh! You tried...

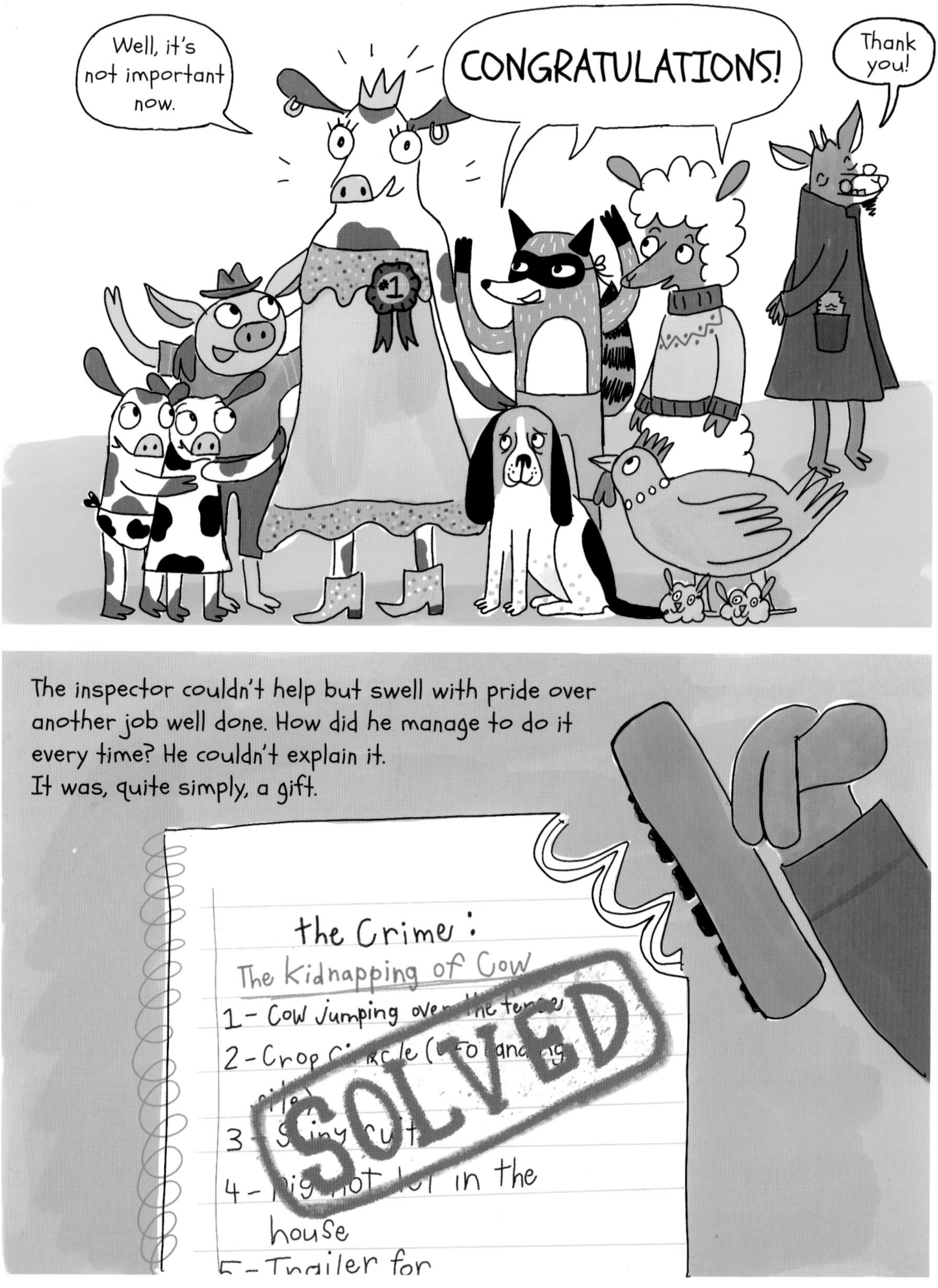
Well, it's not important now.
CONGRATULATIONS!
Thank you!
The inspector couldn't help but swell with pride over another job well done. How did he manage to do it every time? He couldn't explain it.
It was, quite simply, a gift.
the Crime :
The kidnapping of Cow
1 – Cow jumping
2 – Crop
3 –
4 – in the
house
5 – Trailer for
SOLVED

The animals gathered to enjoy a corn roast and to hear all about Cow's success at the fair.

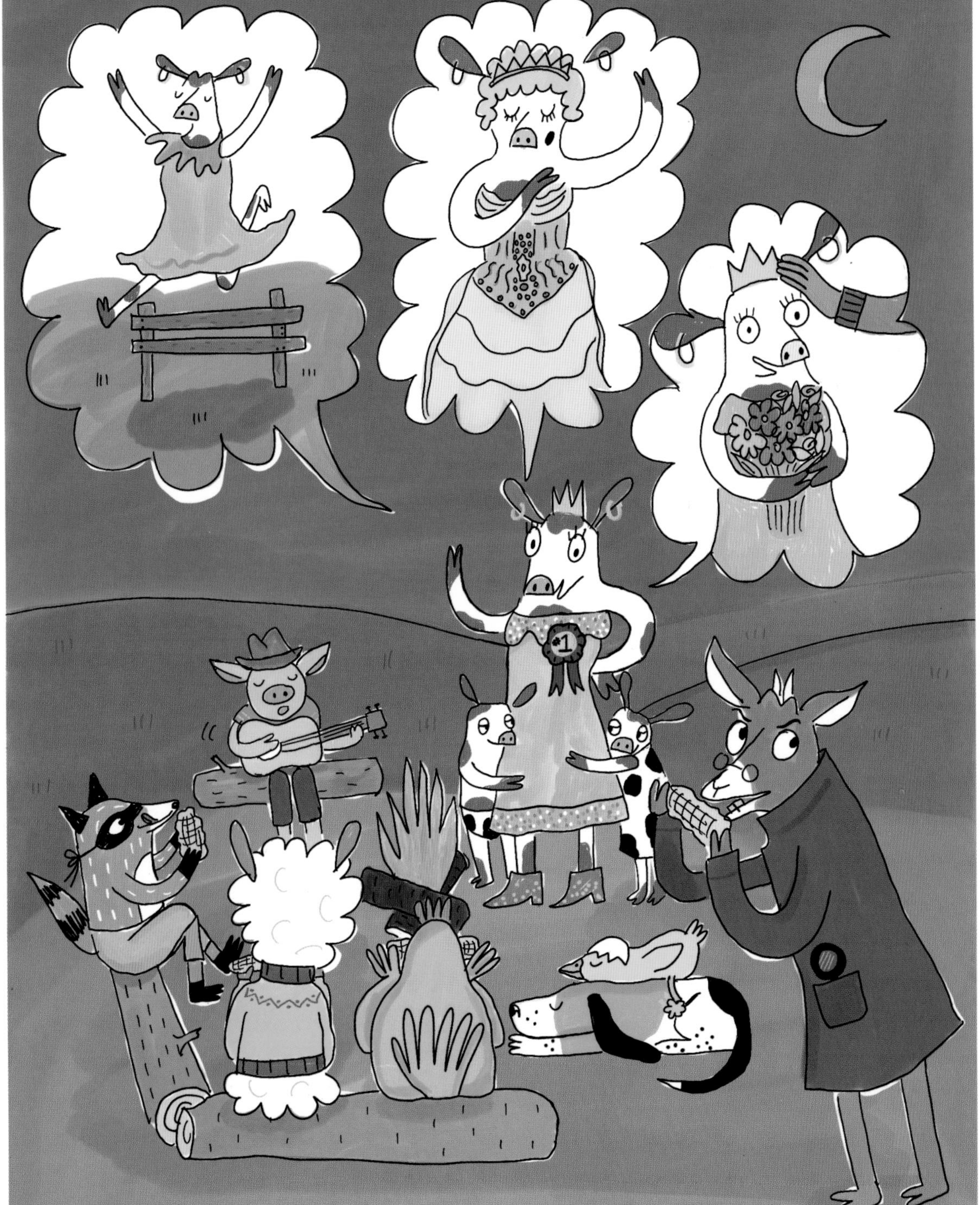
#1

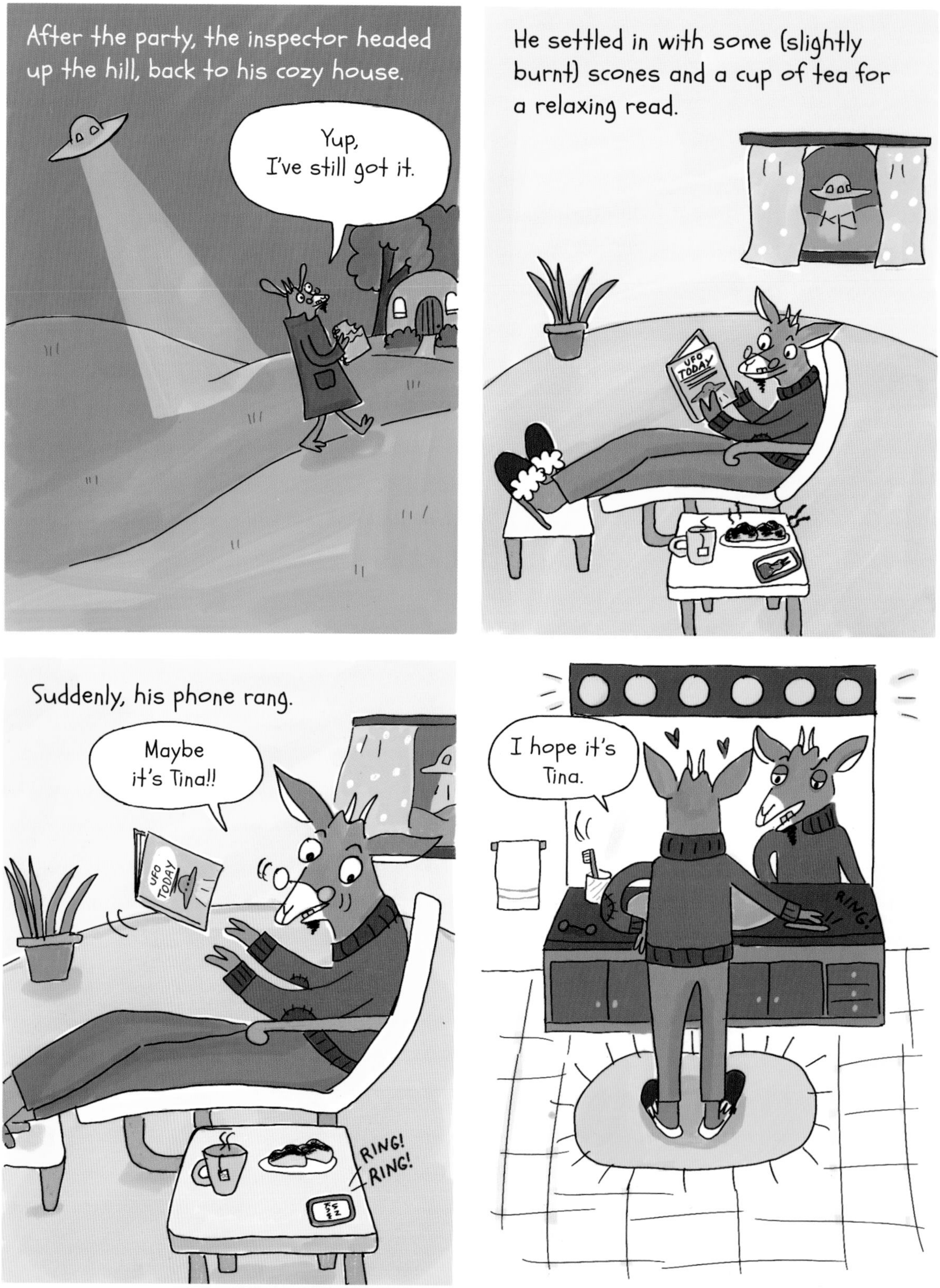
After the party, the inspector headed up the hill, back to his cozy house.
Yup, I've still got it.
He settled in with some (slightly burnt) scones and a cup of tea for a relaxing read.
UFO TODAY
Suddenly, his phone rang.
Maybe it's Tina!!
UFO TODAY
RING! RING!
I hope it's Tina.
RING!

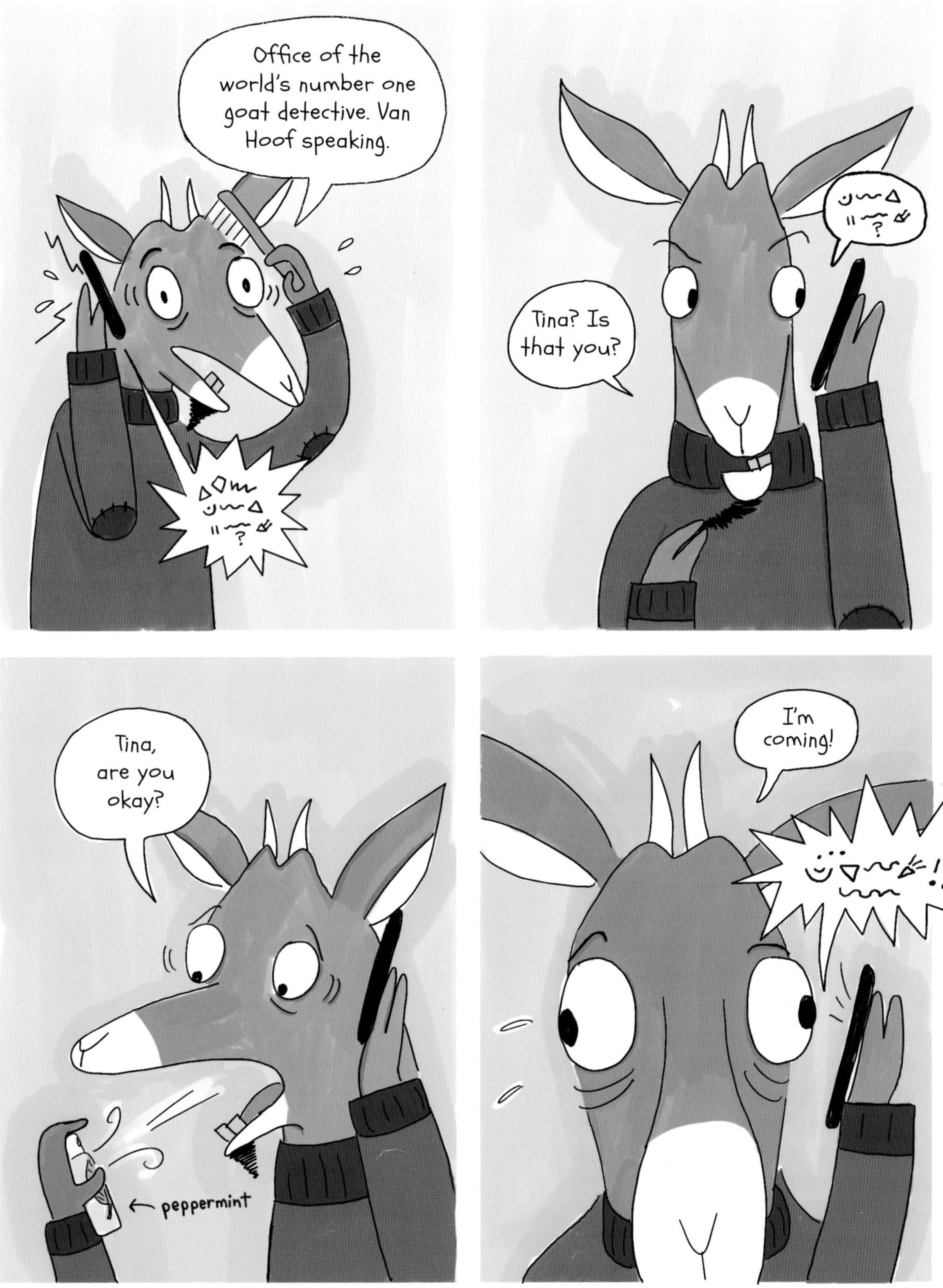
Office of the world's number one goat detective. Van Hoof speaking.
Tina? Is that you?
Tina, are you okay?
peppermint
I'm coming!

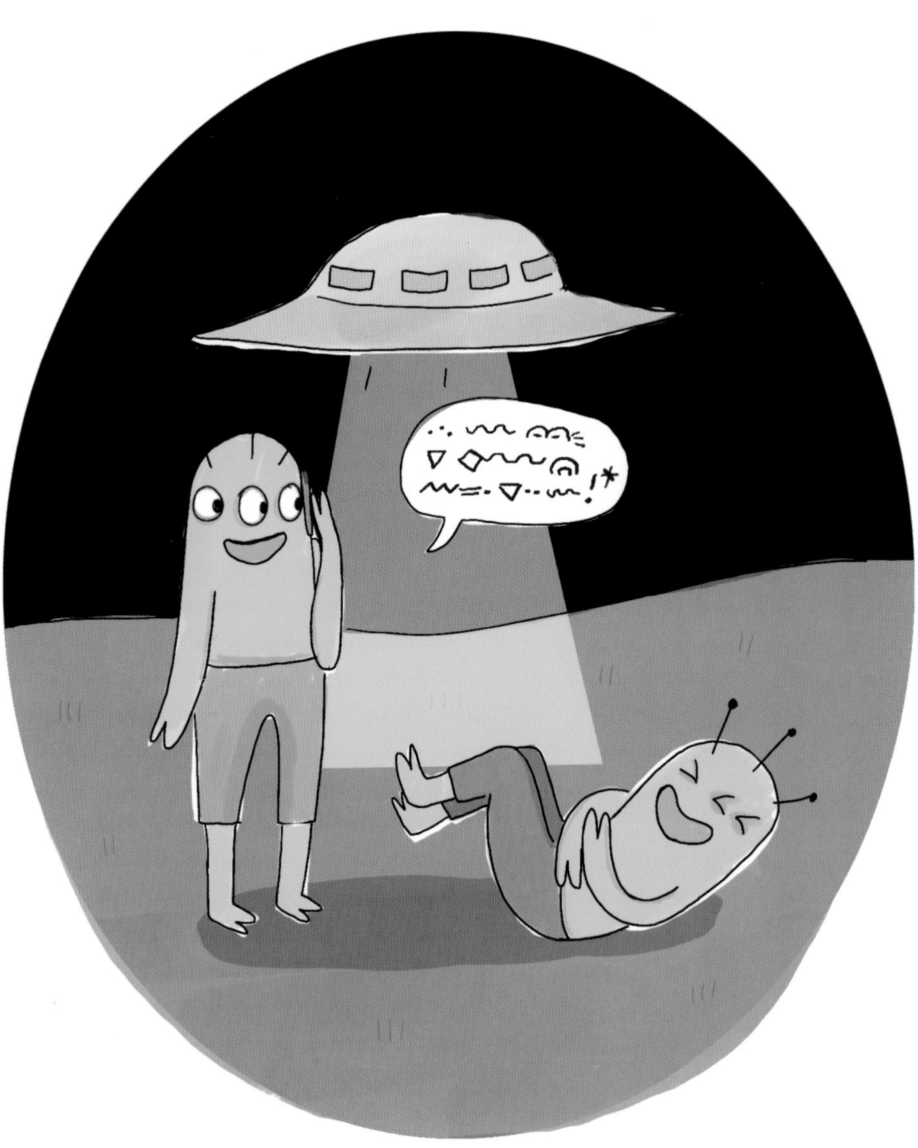

* Hello, I'd like to order a pizza.

Inspector Van Hoof

When not solving mysteries, Billiam Van Hoof enjoys baking, napping, and volunteering at his local chapter of the National Beekeepers' Association.
*He is well known for having a sweet tooth.
*Actually he has two.

Sandra Dumais

When not making books, Sandra Dumais can be found on long snowy walks in Montreal with her husband, two kids, and their rescue dog, Indy. She also teaches art and painting to kids and the young at heart.

Text and illustrations © 2020 Les éditions la courte échelle

Translation © 2021 Sandra Dumais

Original edition published in French under the title *Crimes à la ferme: la mystérieuse disparition de Vache* by la courte échelle, an imprint of Groupe d'édition la courte échelle inc.

Owlkids Books acknowledges the financial support of the Canada Council for the Arts, the Ontario Arts Council, the Government of Canada through the Canada Book Fund (CBF) and the Government of Ontario through the Ontario Creates Book Initiative for our publishing activities.

Published in Canada by
Owlkids Books Inc.
1 Eglinton Avenue East
Toronto, ON M4P 3A1

Published in the United States by
Owlkids Books Inc.
1700 Fourth Street
Berkeley, CA 94710

Library of Congress Control Number: 2020951735

Library and Archives Canada Cataloguing in Publication

Title: Farm crimes! : the moo-sterious disappearance of Cow / Sandra Dumais.
Other titles: Crimes à la ferme, la mystérieuse disparition de Vache. English | Moo-sterious disappearance of Cow | Farm crimes! : the mysterious disappearance of Cow | Mysterious disappearance of Cow
Names: Dumais, Sandra, 1977- author, artist, translator.
Description: Translation of: Crimes à la ferme, la mystérieuse disparition de Vache.
Identifiers: Canadiana 20200414100 | ISBN 9781771474429 (hardcover)
Subjects: LCGFT: Graphic novels.
Classification: LCC PN6733.D835 C7513 2021 | DDC j741.5/971—dc23

ONTARIO ARTS COUNCIL
CONSEIL DES ARTS DE L'ONTARIO
an Ontario government agency
un organisme du gouvernement de l'Ontario

Canada Council
for the Arts
Conseil des Arts
du Canada

Canadä

Manufactured in Guangdong Province, Dongguan City, China, in April 2021, by Toppan Leefung Packaging & Printing (Dongguan) Co., Ltd.   Job # BAYDC91

MIX
Paper from responsible sources
FSC® C104723

A   B   C   D   E   F   G

Publisher of Chirp, Chickadee and OWL
www.owlkidsbooks.com
| Owlkids Books is a division of

bayard canada